Rustomji Pestonji Karkaria

India, Forty Years of Progress and Reform

Being a Sketch of the Life and Times of Behramji M. Malabari

Rustomji Pestonji Karkaria

India, Forty Years of Progress and Reform
Being a Sketch of the Life and Times of Behramji M. Malabari

ISBN/EAN: 9783337096267

Printed in Europe, USA, Canada, Australia, Japan

Cover: Foto ©Raphael Reischuk / pixelio.de

More available books at **www.hansebooks.com**

INDIA

FORTY YEARS OF PROGRESS AND REFORM

BEING

A SKETCH OF THE LIFE AND TIMES OF
BEHRAMJI M. MALABARI

BY

R. P. KARKARIA

EDITOR OF
CARLYLE'S UNPUBLISHED LECTURES ON EUROPEAN LITERATURE
AND CULTURE

London
HENRY FROWDE
OXFORD UNIVERSITY PRESS WAREHOUSE
AMEN CORNER, E.C.

† 1896

PREFACE

In the following pages an attempt has been made to present to the reader a slight sketch of an Indian career which deserves to be known more widely. Mr. Malabari is already well known, both in this country and in Europe, by his own literary works as well as, recently, by the excellent life of him, written by his friend and colleague, Mr. Dayaram Gidumal, C. S.; but above all, by his efforts in the cause of Social Reform. These efforts give him a unique place in contemporary history. The single-minded, straightforward honesty of purpose, the boldness and perseverance shown in the good cause, and, more than all, the spirit of self-sacrifice which pervades his crusade against evils that stand in the way of national progress, stamp him as an exemplary character. His intellectual endowments are great, but they are shared by others among his more prominent countrymen. What raises him above most of his contemporaries is that he combines this intellectual eminence with moral greatness, and subordinates it to a high moral purpose. This is what renders him 'the best among the men whom India is producing in the course of her new development' under British rule. He is the type of true culture, and he has striven hard to leave the world the better for his having entered it. He has had fixed ideals in life, which he has pursued steadily through good report and ill report, allowing

> ' Neither evil tongues,
> Rash judgements, nor the sneers of selfish men, nor all
> The dreary intercourse of daily life[1],'

to prevail over him and make him swerve from the path of Duty, which, in his case, is the path of active benevolence. The life of such a man will be well worth recounting at length, when it has run its full course. Long may that day be in coming! Meanwhile, I have endeavoured to give this outline sketch, based on known facts, with such reflections as suggested themselves while writing about one whom I am proud to call my countryman and friend, whom I had learnt to admire long before I came to know him personally, and personal contact with whom has not only confirmed and increased my admiration for his character and genius, but has made me, I believe, a wiser and a better man. May these slight pages succeed in introducing readers to a great personality, make Indians appreciate better what a force for good they possess in him, and Englishmen rejoice how fruitful the efforts of their race for the mental and moral improvement of this God-given dependency must prove when they produce men like Mr. Malabari.

R. P. KARKARIA.

MATHERAN (near BOMBAY),
    May 9, 1894.

---

[1] Wordsworth, *Lines on Tintern Abbey.*

CONTENTS

————

CHAPTER I.

Contents.

INDIA:

FORTY YEARS OF PROGRESS AND REFORM.

CHAPTER I.

Introduction—The Idea of Self-sacrifice in the East and in the West—
England's Work in India—The System of Education, Western as opposed
to Oriental.

IT is often said that the East has been deficient in
the practice of self-sacrifice, and that instances of lives
of pure philanthropy, devoted to doing good to one's
fellows, without thought of self, are rare in the annals
of Oriental biography. In most books of exemplary
biography, it is the lives of European worthies that
are taken up to point the moral of heroic self-abnega-
tion and the devotion of man to his kind. To a certain
extent this may be owing to the general ignorance
about the East and its affairs and history prevailing
among Europeans. Even when these are inclined to
enlighten themselves on what they have now come
slowly to recognize as the original home of civilization
and the source of light, when they are beginning to
realize the truth of the phrase *ex Oriente lux*, they find
the means at hand rather scanty and unsatisfactory.

B

History, one of the most important branches of knowledge, has been very poorly treated by the Easterns.
By the Hindus of ancient and mediaeval India it was
almost entirely neglected, and with the exception of
two books the whole of Sanskrit literature is barren in
works relating explicitly to facts and events in the life
of the country.   The Mahomedans paid a little more
attention to history, and their literature contains many
works on the subject.   But, unfortunately, they held
peculiar views about the dignity of history, con-
cerning themselves mostly with kings and kingdoms,
recording worldly greatness, but evincing little interest
in the ordinary people and their benefactors.   Hence
their works are full of the details of battles and sieges,
and contain minute particulars about the lives of kings
and conquerors.   Their professed biographies too,
which are few in number, are devoted to men who
have occupied thrones and led conquering hosts.   But
it is not among such that we expect self-denial and
love of others.   On the contrary, from their point of
view they often give us a very low and false idea of
their times.   What a false and mutilated idea should
we have of England in the last century if we had the
record of no other lives than those of Marlborough
and the first two Georges, and nothing to remind us
of the career of Wesley and Howard!   Such an idea
of the East is carried away by those who read the
history of Tamarlane and Jenghis Khan, of Mahmud
of Ghazni and Aurangzib of Delhi.   The redeeming
features presented by the silent lives of good men
working for the benefit of their fellows, are generally

absent in Mahomedan literature, and are apt to be inferred as having not existed at all.

But in truth, the East has been the home of the doctrine of self-sacrifice since the earliest times. It has been the birthplace of all the great religions which are founded on the subordination or the effacement of self with regard to one's Maker and his kind. Zoroastrianism, probably the oldest of religions, has for its cardinal doctrine that of charity and doing good to mankind without thought of self. The system of Buddha, which has profoundly and permanently affected the greater half of the Eastern world, is based on self-effacement and tender consideration, not only for the human race, but the entire living creation. The life of the noble enthusiast himself is one of the most striking instances of careers devoted with an unswerving singleness of purpose to benefit the world. Hinduism, too, though in its later Brahmanic development it has become a selfish and exclusive cult hedged round by caste, is, in its origin and essence, an inspiriting faith. Manu's beautiful idea of original debt, implying that every man is born a debtor, and must discharge his original debt by doing good deeds for his fellows, is like the Christian doctrine of original sin, and perhaps more inspiring. And the Christian religion, the noblest, in this respect, of all, having for its central mystery the sacrifice of the second person of the Godhead Himself, for the redemption and final happiness of fallen man, had its birth in the East, in that narrow strip in the corner which unites Europe with Asia, symbolic of the spiritual union of the two great continents to be effected through its agency. Jesus Himself, the highest type of self-sacrifice, was born an Asiatic; and His life, though lived for the whole world, was spent on Asiatic soil amid Oriental surroundings. Of Islam, the latest of the world religions, the fundamental idea is resignation of one's will and self-surrender, though that ideal has been clouded by many contradictory practices in the course of its development. And it is not merely in the lives of the founders of these world-religions that we find the doctrine of self-sacrifice and its practice. All of them have produced heroic characters, who have lived and died solely for their fellow-beings. But the saying, that the world does not know its greatest men, is true at least of the East, which has kept a very meagre record of the lives and deeds of its really great men.

It may however be admitted, that the ideal pursued by the East in this matter of self-sacrifice has been chiefly a subjective one. With its traditional propensity to metaphysics and contemplation, it has been more or less content with practising self-sacrifice in a passive way, giving itself up to austerity and self-communion, and detaching itself from the world. Thus it has been the chosen cradle and home of Rishis and Fakirs, who have tried to efface self by solitary meditation on spiritual matters. Hence it has also been the birthplace of monasticism, Buddhist and Christian, in which the soul, full too much of self, sought a refuge in surrendering itself passively to a higher ideal. The West has been, on the contrary, practical and active in the matter. Its ideal has been action and movement, while that of the East has been quiet and rest. It has received the doctrine of self-sacrifice from the East, and has modified it according to its bent, and made it practical and active. Hence in modern times in Europe we see men sacrificing themselves, not by detachment and seclusion from the world, but by leading active lives of usefulness in and for the world. The passive Eastern ideal, which was also preferred by Aristotle and mediaeval Europe, has to a great extent given way to the progress of positive science, and has, in modern Europe, become active for bettering man's estate. Instead of monks leading a cloistered life away from the din of the world, we now have monks of a higher order, pursuing an equally noble ideal in the very thick of life, trying to alleviate human misery, and instead of retiring from the field of action, standing firmly by the side of their weaker fellows and helping them to fight the battle of life more bravely. The Catholic Church, the great stronghold of monasticism in the Middle Ages, has seen and felt this momentous change of ideal that has come upon modern Europe, and has wisely adapted itself to the change. The institution of the historic order of Jesus, whose members lead an active life of self-sacrifice in the very midst of the world, living thus in full touch with it, is no slight proof of the wisdom and elasticity of the Church of Rome.

The West, having taken this ideal from the East, and having modified it according to its own genius, has tried to return it to the East in this state. The highest ideal of active philanthropy has been attempted by the Teutonic nations, whose very genius lies in action and motion. And it has been the great good fortune of the East to come next in contact with one of the two great branches of the sturdy, active Teutonic races which proved the salvation of Europe in freeing it from the effete and moribund rule of the degenerate Roman empire. This branch, the British, has been destined by a singular fate to affect profoundly one of the most important countries of the East, India, and its ideals. The English have become, in this land, the masters of one of the greatest Oriental empires that ever flourished in ancient or modern times. And they have always tried to use this mastery for the benefit of the subject races. Since the early dawn of their rule, when it was hardly yet established in the country, efforts have been made to raise the people to a higher level by conferring upon them the blessings of Western civilization and culture. The generation that elapsed after Plassey was spent mainly in the struggle for establishing themselves. But when, after conquest and diplomacy, more leisure was left for peaceful pursuits, the English were not slow in utilizing their opportunities for doing good. The results, in the direction of material advance, have been glorious indeed. To him who asks for a monument of the British rule in India, an appropriate answer may be made in the celebrated phrase, *Circumspice!* He has only to look round about him in the land to find permanent memorials of British beneficence. Her highways and railroads and canals; her large and flourishing cities, the centres of her manufactures and trade, developed to proportions hitherto unknown; her gigantic public works,—all these are living monuments of Britain's philanthropic rule of a century, beside which nearly everything done in this line by former dynasties during much longer periods sinks into insignificance. .

But greater even than this triumph of material progress is that of mental and moral advance. (England has had the rare satisfaction of awakening the torpid Hindu intellect from the sleep into which it had been thrown by the fierce foreign rule of the Mahomedans during seven centuries, the real Middle Ages of Indian history.\ In its far-reaching importance this new period of the *Éclaircissement* in modern India may be compared to the awakening of the European mind from the inactivity of the Middle Ages at the time of the Renaissance. As the mind of Western Europe, dazzled by the new stores of Greek learning in the fifteenth century revealed to its admiring gaze by Byzantine scholars, refused to proceed any longer on the old beaten track of mediaeval knowledge, and eagerly followed the new light, striking out new paths of science and philosophy; so the Indian intellect, profoundly moved in many ways, in our century, by the revelation to it of European culture through the English language and literature, is striving after fresh conquests. The revolution which the young Indian mind is experiencing has stirred it powerfully, and its influence is being felt in many departments of life. Slowly but surely the whole fabric of Indian society is

changing under this salutary foreign influence brought
to bear upon it by the alien rulers.

Two agencies were, from the first, employed by
these rulers to achieve their object of ameliorating
the condition of the millions placed under their care
by an all-wise Providence. One was that of active
missionary effort by which the early enthusiasts among
the pioneers of British progress sought to reclaim the
Indians from their old faith. The deep hold which
this faith had upon the people, however absurd it may
have appeared to the followers and inheritors of
a nobler religion, was not realized by the first generation of English philanthropists. The efforts at direct
conversion to Christianity were vigorously put forth,
till it became necessary to acknowledge with bitterness
that as direct efforts they had proved on the whole
futile. It was found that direct and open proselytism
frightened the people and made them averse to
European learning altogether, when coupled with the
European faith. It was feared that this method would
defeat the object of improving the condition of the
people, even intellectually and materially, and give
rise to a reaction in favour not only of the old faith,
but also of the old ways of thinking and living which
were beginning to be visibly affected by the Western
modes. The tenacity and vitality of the indigenous
religions had to be acknowledged and reckoned with.
Even as early as the close of the last century it was
frankly confessed by one of the best missionaries, who
knew the people intimately, and had lived for a long
time as one of themselves, namely, Dubois, that Chris-

tianity was not destined to make headway amongst the Indian nations. It could best succeed but indirectly, as we shall have occasion to remark later, by modifying the indigenous creeds. But it did not seem likely ever to win over the subtle Hindu mind to itself, so as to make that mind accept all its dogmas and mysteries implicitly. Even able officers of the Government were, in the earlier days, carried away by their zeal for the spread of the Gospel, impervious to the force of this observation. Many of them urged the East India Company to exert its influence for the spread of its own faith among the people. One of the ablest men among them, who had really the good of the people at heart, a Director of the Company, thought it wise to write as follows, after mature deliberation and a long and close study of the people. In the Preface to his now very rare *Observations on the State of Society among the Asiatic Subjects of Great Britain*, addressed in 1797 to his fellow Directors, Charles Grant says, 'In earlier periods the Company manifested a laudable zeal for extending, as far as its means then went, the knowledge of the Gospel to the pagan tribes among whom its factories were placed. It has since prospered to become great in a way to which the commercial history of the world affords no parallel, and for this it is indebted to the fostering and protecting care of Divine Providence. It owes, therefore, warmest gratitude for the past, and it equally needs the support of the same beneficent Power in time to come for the "chances and changes" to which human affairs are always liable, and specially the emphatic lessons of vicissitude which the present day has supplied may assure us that neither elevation nor safety can be maintained by any of the nations or rulers of the earth, but through Him who governs the whole.   The duty, therefore, of the Company, as part of the Christian community, its peculiar super-added obligations, its enlarged means, and its continual dependence on the Divine favour, all call upon it to honour God by diffusing the knowledge of that revelation which He has vouchsafed to mankind[1].'

But views like these rapidly give way to increased experience and maturer consideration.   Proselytizing zeal and effort were given up by the Government as an agency for improving the moral and mental condition of the people.   Secular education was preferred for the purpose.   The mind of the people was sought to be enlightened by literary and scientific information. It was hoped that the old creeds would languish of themselves when the light of reason and knowledge was thrown upon them.   The odium of direct attack would thus be averted, and the citadel of superstition would fall by what could be likened to the sapping and mining process.

But here sprang up an important difference among men entrusted with the task of organizing secular education, which threatened seriously to cripple the power of this agency for raising the masses.   Mountstuart Elphinstone, in his famous minute on education, written in 1824, expressed his confident conviction,

[1] Appendix, G. Smith, *Conversion of India*, 1893, p. 99.

while resisting direct missionary effort, that 'the conversion of the natives must infallibly result from the diffusion of knowledge among them' (*Official Writings*, ed. Forrest, page 107). Some among these, being themselves well versed in the Eastern lore, impelled by the desire of fostering indigenous literature and learning, were strongly for imparting knowledge to the Indians in their own classics and vernaculars, and for confining them to their own literatures. These men, who were led by the distinguished Sanskritist, Prof. H. H. Wilson, were very influential, and were once very near carrying their point. Had they succeeded, the result would have been little short of a disaster, throwing back all progress. The Eastern mind would have been thrown upon itself, doomed to tread the narrow range of its indigenous ancient productions. These have undoubtedly their own great merits, and hold a high rank in universal literature. But they must be admitted by even their warmest admirers to be insufficient for modern times and purposes. An exclusive study of these alone would tend to confirm the bent of the Indian intellect in one direction alone, and prevent its acquiring that breadth of view and liberality which is an essential requisite of true culture. When such a rich body of literature existed in the English language, including the masterpieces of the master minds of all ages and all countries of Europe, it would have argued the height of unwisdom deliberately to ignore this language and its literature, with all its variety and freshness, in the face of a splendid opportunity of utilizing them for the rarest of purposes in the gift of one nation, that of raising another, with an earlier civilization, but now sunk in the scale of humanity. Luckily, a man was on the spot, who, himself thoroughly imbued with the modern spirit, stood up for the spread of modern culture and learning. Macaulay threw the whole weight of his influence and all his great powers of persuasion on the side of imparting an English and European education to the natives of India, and he won the battle. He wrote, in his most persuasive manner, a minute which is in reality an essay, superior in many respects to his professed popular essays, and gained over the Governor-General, Lord Bentinck.

More than sixty years have elapsed since this momentous decision, and during these a revolution has been working in the country, which is really marvellous to witness, and unparalleled in the history of conquests. When Rome, by her material strength, had subdued Greece, the mother of arts and eloquence, she herself fell an easy victim to the mental strength of her captive. *Graecia capta ferum victorem cepit.* Grecian learning and literature were adopted by Rome. Her great writers imitated the Greeks, and their works are often but an echo of Hellenic literature. But England may be said to have achieved a double triumph over India, of which she has captured both mind and matter. Far from being Asiaticized and Hinduized by this conquest, she has succeeded in Europeanizing and Anglicizing the Indian mind. The seed of Western culture has so far fallen on fertile soil, and is already producing a rich harvest.

Dr. Arnold, in one of his Lectures on Modern History, after the striking observation that the changes which have been wrought in the world have arisen out of the reception of the old elements of progress by new races, despaired of any further advance owing to the absence, in his eyes, of any new race capable of receiving such old elements. ' Now, looking anxiously round the world for any new races which may receive the seed (so to speak) of our present history into a kindly yet vigorous soil, and may reproduce it, the same, and yet new, for a future period, we know not where such are to be found. Some appear exhausted, others incapable, and yet the surface of the whole globe is thrown open to us.' Little did Arnold dream while uttering these gloomy words in 1842, that at that very time the seed was being sown on fertile soil in India by his countrymen rightly refusing to believe that the Indians were either exhausted or incapable [1]. Macaulay and Bentinck were justified in their expectation of the enormous benefits to accrue to the Indian races from English education. During the last two generations India has gone through a new and a unique development, fraught with momentous consequences to itself and to the British Empire. Under Western influences the former traditional moorings are already being gradually left behind, and the educated classes are drifting towards another goal. The new system of

[1] Cp. Hay Cameron, *Duties of Britain to India*, p. 127.

education has produced a race of capable and earnest natives of the soil, imbued with the Western spirit and possessed by the zeal to pursue higher ideals in life, more in harmony with the times. It is of one of the ablest and most brilliant men of this new class, which owes its existence to the noble motive and fostering care of the British rule, that this sketch purposes to treat. That man, the best, as Sir John Scott, who knew him well while in Bombay, describes him, whom India in the course of her new development has produced, is Behramji Malabari, poet, publicist, author, but above everything else, philanthropist and social reformer. Or rather, it may be said that he is poet, publicist and other things, solely and almost exclusively for the purpose of being a philanthropist and social reformer.

Most of these English educated Indians have thought it wise to choose the sphere of politics for the exercise of their newly-acquired strength. Of all the various kinds of activity which they have seen exercised by public men in the West, and especially in England, they have been dazzled by the most brilliant as exhibited in the field of politics. Nurtured on the liberal sentiments and lofty notions which are the distinguishing features of English literature, they have naturally been impelled, in the first instance, to apply these to their own country, though a closer knowledge of its past history and present condition would have advised them better. Their activities have been engrossed by a burning desire for the reform of the State, and to this object they are sacrificing all others.

This tendency was observed in the newly-educated
natives from the very beginning, and there were many
who were apprehensive of grave political danger from
such a system of education.   Lord Ellenborough, for
instance, in his evidence before the Committee of the
House of Commons, openly and emphatically declared
his opinion that if. endeavours were made to impart
European education and ideas to the natives, the
English must not expect to retain their hold on India.
But other high-minded Englishmen were not wanting
to come forward and defend the generous course
which it had been decided to pursue, of enabling the
Indians to develop to the utmost the good qualities
with which Providence had endowed them from the
earliest times, and of raising them by the lever of
a liberal European education from the depths into
which they had fallen in the course of prolonged
subjugation, especially under Mahomedan rule.   Even
from a selfish point of view it was pointed out that
England should rejoice at this education of the natives.
'The class that we are creating,' wrote Mr. Hay
Cameron, one of the most enlightened champions of
native progress in these early days, 'as we approach
towards this great object, the class imbued with
European letters, will be for many generations wholly
dependent upon us, much more so than any of the
separate and antagonistic classes which we found
already existing ; and they will exceed all these other
classes in their enlightened perception of their true
position, still more than in the degree of dependence
which characterizes it.   They know that, if we were

voluntarily to retire from India, they would instantly be subjugated by fierce and unlettered warriors [1].' Two generations have now gone by, and the lettered class, contemplated here, has grown up with the growth and strengthened with the strength of the British Empire in India, as its proudest and most lasting trophy. Whatever may be thought of the exclusive or one-sided activity of certain among our native politicians of the present day, it cannot be denied that they are a powerful factor in their way, who only require to be properly treated and utilized by the rulers, to do all that was expected from them, and be a source of strength, rather than of weakness, to the Government that has made their existence possible.

Of all the objections that are raised against this new class of politicians, who restrict their energies to a close watching of the acts of the British Government and subjecting these to minute, if not sometimes *captious* criticism, the strongest, because most reasonable, seems to be that they are not utilizing their newly-acquired strength in the direction which requires it most, in trying to remove those crying evils which infest the social side of the body politic, and which stand so much in the way of realizing their new political ideals. The present *régime* may be bad—though it has by no means been proved that it is not immeasurably superior to the best under which India has hitherto lived. Its acts now and then deserve censure. But the present social condition of the people, characterized,

[1] *Duties of Britain to India,* 1853, p. 51.

as it is, by senseless and inhuman customs, undermining their vitality and debasing their ideals, is admittedly worse. If there be any one task which should absorb the energy of the educated class, and in which they should seek for help from every available quarter, it is this of moral and social reform. The State is based on the family, and before trying to reform the former, attempts must be made to improve the latter. 'The inner life of the people and their homes must be made healthy, morally and physically, before any solid improvement of the outer life is attempted.' A people with their homes debased, their women ignorant and superstitious, a people trammelled with all the old-world prejudices and subject to the most cruelly one-sided customs and usages, can never hope to enjoy or exercise high political privileges. All endeavours in this direction alone, without fulfilling the preliminary conditions of moral and social reform, must end in disappointment if not in disaster.

This great need of social reform, though ignored apparently by the body of educated natives, has yet been felt by a few of the most enlightened among them. They know the evil customs that have settled like a blight upon their race, destroying its vitality and arresting its progress, and are conscious of the splendid opportunity, afforded by the British protectorate, of getting rid of these customs. They feel the importance of the advice given by experienced and thoughtful Englishmen, like Sir Alfred Lyall, who work to advance their welfare and to see it really advanced to a certain extent by themselves. 'We may hope that all reflect-

ing and far-sighted natives of that class, which we are
rapidly training up in large towns in political knowledge
and social freedom, will perceive that England's prime
function in India is at present this, to superintend the
tranquil elevation of the whole moral and intellectual
standard.   Those who are interested in such a change
in the ethics of their country, in broadening the realms
of the known and the true, must see how ruinously
premature it is to quarrel with the English Government upon details of administration, or even upon
what are called constitutional questions [1].'

Being convinced of the good intentions of the
British Government and its desire to elevate the people,
the minority we are speaking of use their strength to
help forward its efforts and to extract as much out of
the present favourable times as possible for the social
and moral advancement of the people.   With this
conviction always before them, they labour earnestly
for their countrymen and women in every province of
this vast land.   They are a small band, working in
harmony, though scattered over the continent, and at
a great sacrifice of time and resources.   Working
incessantly, they have formed a movement within
a few years, which, for its far-reaching usefulness, rivals
any of the more attractive agencies started by the
more popular political party.   For their lofty purpose,
their disinterested efforts on behalf of the weak and
the suffering, and their personal sacrifices, they may
well be compared to the famous group of philanthropists
whom Sir James Stephen has popularized by the name

[1] *Asiatic Studies*, p. 305.

of the Clapham Sect, and who fought so valiantly, persistently, and at last successfully for the emancipation of slaves about the beginning of this century. Of nothing could England be more justly proud than of having been the means of organizing this small band of reformers in India, imbued not only with the literature and learning, but also with the real Christian charity of the West.

At the head of these stands the subject of our sketch, who has used all his great gifts for the advancement of the cause, the vital importance of which he was really the first to recognize, and which, but for him, it is not too much to say, would never have obtained its now universal recognition. How he realized social reform as the one great task of his life, devoting to it everything in his power, and making for it sacrifices which alone stamp him as a rare character in a self-seeking age; how, from a hopeless and discredited cause, ridiculed as utterly impracticable, he gave to it its proper place as the burning question of the day, involving the happiness of millions, and changed almost entirely in its favour the current of the influential opinion which at first ran against it; and how, when he finally succeeded in rousing the authorities to a due sense of their responsibility in the matter, and in obtaining a legislative measure of relief which, though small at present, may develop later into much larger proportions; how he met the obloquy and misrepresentation of those very classes whom he had devoted his life to benefit,—all this we may now proceed briefly to narrate.

CHAPTER II.

BEHRAMJI MALABARI was born in the year 1853-4, in the city of Baroda, the capital of the Gaikwad, one of the surviving group of rulers who formed in the last century the much-dreaded Mahratta confederacy. His father was Dhanjibhai Mehta, a clerk in the service of the State, who died, leaving his widow and child in a helpless condition. Dhanjibhai Mehta does not seem to have been of much help to the family even when alive, as owing to differences with other members of the 'joint family,' his wife had to leave her husband's house at Baroda and go to settle again in her birth-place, Surat, with her little child of two. This journey, which is now performed in about three hours by rail, was even so lately as forty years ago fraught with peculiar difficulties and danger. The Gaikwad govern-ment has only recently passed into strong hands, able and willing to protect the people from lawlessness. Under former administrations the territories were infested by wild tribes, and travelling was very unsafe. Bhils, Girasias, and Pindaris, who were the terror and

the curse of Western and Central India, even under
the British, till eighty years ago, when, by an organized
effort, they were run down and their power broken by
the Marquis of Hastings, still survived in the native
States, that had probably connived at, if not actually
encouraged, their rise. Old men in the Gaikwad
territories still recall with a shudder the terrible
periodic raids of these banditti, made in open defiance
of all lawful authority, and sweeping away in their
merciless career men, women and children, cattle and
crop alike. These raids are not quite unknown even
now in some native States, notably Kathiawad, which
is perhaps the last resort of the banditti, as its jungles
contain the only lions to be found in Western India.
It was a party of one of these lawless tribes, the Bhils,
that fell in with the poor exile from her husband's home,
just out of her teens, and laden with her precious
charge, the little boy of two, in a hay-cart. But they
who came to plunder, and possibly to kill, remained to
caress the child and protect the mother, undertaking
to send them safe to their destination with presents
for both!

The narrative of this lucky escape, says Malabari,
'was repeated to me by my mother whenever I was
ill, after which both of us prayed to God.' This is
a characteristic trait, early developed and always the
strongest, in his character. He is, above everything,
prayerful, a 'prayerful poet,' with the religious sentiment prominent and largely cultivated. His writings
show this abundantly. But the trait is still better
illustrated by his whole life, which is a beautiful

instance of religious culture. This he seems to have inherited from his mother, no ordinary woman, but one quite worthy of such an extraordinary character as her son has proved himself to be. Indeed, as the son is never tired of repeating, without such a mother he would not have been what he is. Apart from hereditary influences, which are subtle and elude close analysis, it was his environment during tender years, the close communion in which he lived with such a mother, that probably gave the bent to his life, which he has followed throughout, emerging at last as an active philanthropist, undaunted by dangers and difficulties, or rather seeking these for the sake of overcoming them. The mother, who had the courage to leave home, under persecution, travel through deadly dangers with her little son at her breast in a hay-cart, and set up for herself in a new town, with 'the world all before her where to choose, and Providence her guide'; the mother that considered all the boys in the street her own sons, and refused to save the life of her own child on a critical occasion by imperilling that of the child of another and a stranger, was surely worthy of a son who has undertaken to champion the cause of women as of his own mother and sisters and daughters, and who has, for this self-imposed task, put up with obloquy and insult, has seen his purest motives questioned and unworthy ones imputed, without ever swerving from the path of duty.

Bhikhibai was, indeed, a remarkable woman, whom her son resembles physically as well as morally. Her short stature, light complexion, roundish face, and large,

far-looking eyes, may be traced more or less in him.
That she was a strong-minded and firm-willed woman,
we have already seen.   But she had as soft and large
a heart, with tender feelings for all, regardless of creed
or colour, as she had a strong mind and firm will.
She tried to be useful in her humble sphere, with her
limited resources, and left her mark on the little circle
in which she moved.   She had, in common with other
women of her class, some knowledge of herbs, which
she was ever ready to impart to her neighbours in
trouble, who also found in her a willing and ready
helpmate and an excellent adviser.   Nor was she
swayed by any narrow exclusive ideas of her duty.
Though a Parsi, she mixed freely with Hindus,
without imbibing any of the rigid caste prejudices of
the latter.   She once took up tenderly a half-dead
infant, lying in a basket near her door, and at once
put it to her breast without inquiring as to its caste, as
nearly every Indian woman would have done.   The
infant turned out to be of the lowest caste, that of
Mahars or sweepers; and she had, for some time after,
to bear the raillery and taunts of her Parsi neighbours.
On another occasion, when her beloved son was stricken
with small-pox, and on the point of death, she refused
to listen to a quack, who advised her, as the only way
of saving her son, to cut off the live nails and eye-
brows of another boy, and offer them as an appeasing
sacrifice to the goddess of small-pox : in India there
are gods and goddesses of everything, even of diseases.
Though tremblingly anxious for the recovery of her
son, who was her all-in-all, Bhikhibai would not employ

such cruel means as to endanger the life of another's
son even to save her own. 'All the boys in the street
are my own sons,' she generously cried out, even in
her extreme anxiety to save her own. And she had
the reward of her generosity. Her son recovered,
when, as usual with her, she offered a sacrifice of
grateful prayers to her living God.

Such was Bhikhibai. Her son has celebrated her
virtues in prose and verse. 'What a mother mine
was!' he writes in one place, 'a picture of self-sacrifice.
Some people live to die; others are prepared to die,
so that they may live. My mother was one of these.
She died at thirty-three, but still she lives in the
memory of many who knew her. To me she has been
and will be alive always. How can a mother die?
There is an aroma of immortality about the word
Mother and the idea it clothes ... I carry my mother
about in the spirit. She is always present to me. In
every good woman I see my mother; I pity every bad
or ill-used woman for my mother's sake.'

A few years after Bhikhibai's arrival at Surat she
had to marry again, a relative, Merwanji Malabari by
name, who adopted her son, and whose name has now
been made a household word throughout India. This
marriage was contracted partly that the adoptive
father might be of worldly use to her son, and partly
to help her parents. But, as might be expected, it
turned out unhappy. Merwanji had a druggist's shop,
and dealt in sandalwood and spices imported by him
from the Malabar coast, which accounts for his surname
of Malabari. At first he appears to have been in easy

circumstances, but owing to the loss of a ship he was
reduced to straits. Thus the mother's hope of his
being useful to her son was frustrated, and the boy had
to undergo a severe apprenticeship of life very early.
The stepfather, though he survived his wife long and
died about ten years ago, was of very little help to
the boy. During the first twelve years of his life
Behramji was entirely under the care of his mother,
who did her best to mould his genius and to render
sober and steady his wandering habits. This maternal
influence of Bhikhibai may be likened to that which
Goethe's mother, Frau Aja, had on that great man's
stormy boyhood and early life. Goethe, too, was a
man of strong passions and stubborn will, and having
lost his father's control early, had to depend upon the
mother's guidance. Bhikhibai, like Frau Aja, was
a woman of strong individuality and common sense,
and knew, in her own humble way, how to mould the
character of her wayward son.

During these twelve years, the period of his boyhood—for, as we shall see, his manhood began soon.
after—he seems to have led a sort of Bohemian life,
going from school to school, changing one eccentric
teacher for another, and learning little in a methodic
way from his books. But he learnt what was of greater
importance to him, perhaps, in after life—to observe
men and their ways, and to take a keen interest in
human affairs. The pictures which he has drawn of
his early teachers and companions show that even then
he had begun to observe and study his fellows, and
what is more, to make allowance for their weaknesses

and shortcomings. A very kindly tone pervades these sketches; and even when wronged, he guards himself against being unjust. Indeed, the wonder is, that having so early passed through such gloomy and embittering phases of life as he depicts, he has not become a cynic, as would have been the case with most. He has rather become more tolerant, and all the readier to find redeeming features in dark spots. Even of such a wild bully as his first Parsi teacher, and a tyrant like his next Hindu preceptor, he has many kind things to say. Then he had also some objectionable companions, which was but natural in a school where very little discrimination is shown in herding together the scholars. But he had, also, some softening influence in the companionship of a spiritually minded girl who was, he says, the dearest friend he had in his school-days. Another powerful influence exercised on him then was that of the peculiar poetry of the Khialis, itinerant bards, who were well known in Gujarat until within a few years ago. Like the troubadours and trouveurs of France, and the minnesingers of Germany, they travelled about from place to place, leading a semi-ascetic life, and dependent on alms, gaining a precarious livelihood by their voice and instruments. Though much of their language was Hindi, they were singularly liberal in their views, which were eclectic and free from the narrowness of creed and country. Their poetry was originally meta-physical and pure, and some of the best ethical songs in the Gujarati language have been composed by these bards. But in course of time it has degenerated into

materialism and even sensualism. The later generations of these bards indulged more or less in ribaldry;
and the original philosophical sects among them, which
had risen owing to speculative differences, degenerated
into parties who often used much more material
arguments than figures and syllogisms, and generally
ended their discussions in street brawls, in which the
hand, and not the head, had a prominent part. Surat
was, in Malabari's early days, frequented by these
minstrels; and by his musical tastes, and still more
perhaps by his Bohemian habits, he was soon attracted
towards them. He was sometimes involved in the
vortex of their rowdy tournaments, and enjoyed the
music as well as the fun of broken head and lacerated
skin. But he had caught the genuine poetic inspiration from the songs of the earlier bards, whose masterpieces he studied and imitated. Malabari came out
as a poet in Gujarati, his mother-tongue, and the
poetical instinct was roused in him by these street
bards of Surat. The strong ethical bias in his poetry
is chiefly due to his serious nature, which loves to
ponder on the realities of life and its complex problems.
But it is also partly owing to the study of these older
lyrics. There are many such in his first volume of
Gujarat verse, whose title shows the preponderance
of the ethical element, *Niti-Vinod*. His latest book of
verse, in his mother-tongue, is also ethical and philosophical, and shows traces still of his early passion for
the vagaries of the itinerant bards.

Thus gay as well as unconsciously grave, he was
passing his early years in apparent ease, as also amid

some difficulties, under the protection of his mother. She knew the weakness of her son, and tried earnestly to steady him and to wean him from his wandering habits. She grieved at his passion for music, which threatened to outrun all limits and to lead him into keeping objectionable company. Having a very sweet voice, of rare compass, the boy was much in request with the singers, and in this the mother must have discerned a peculiar danger. She, however, brought him round by affectionate reasoning, and made him promise—a promise since faithfully kept—never to sing in public, nor associate with the bards. She had also detected in him a tendency to drink, borrowed unconsciously from some of his thoughtless companions. To break this habit in time she confronted the boy with a ghastly object-lesson, the sight of an unfortunate woman lying on her back near the city gate, dead drunk, towards the evening. The mother, with her usual charity, sent her boy to fetch some curdled milk, a popular antidote for drunkenness, and reluctantly left the woman after having thrust the milk down her throat and turned her into a more decent posture. That sight must have cured the boy on the spot.

Thus the mother was his good genius during her lifetime. And she continued to be more so after her death. She was stricken down by cholera, dying in her thirty-third year, leaving her son in his twelfth, alone and absolutely friendless. The stroke came swift, sudden, and heavy. It cut his life into twain. With his mother he bade farewell to his boyhood, his frivolities and indiscretion, and became at once and for ever a *man*. As he has himself sung in touching verse,

'She clasped a child, with sad emotions wan,
    But when the clasp relaxed, there was left a man.'

His mother's death, so terrible a blow in itself, had, however, a chastening influence upon him, and settled his wavering mind. Nothing that she did in life for him—and what did she *not* do ?—was so important to his future prospects as her death. It came at a critical moment of his mental and moral development, which henceforward seems to have proceeded in a regular sober order. Malabari is undoubtedly a genius : one has only to come in contact with him to discover this, if indeed it is not patent through his works. But there was a risk, as in most such cases, of this erratic genius failing to find its true sphere of activity, and either becoming perverted, or frittering itself away in obscurity and inanition. Those who know him as he now is can hardly realize that this shy, shrinking, self-denying friend of theirs should ever have been a forward, aggressive, self-asserting street-boy, ringleader in many a frolic, and always to the fore where risk and fun alike were to be faced. But the lives of great men afford many instances of this kind of sudden transformation. Augustine is, perhaps, the most notable instance in point. From a youth, wholly abandoned to the world and its vicious ways, taking life easily and thinking of little beyond the enjoyment of the moment, he suddenly, as if by miraculous interposition, became serious and pious, weighed down heavily by the stern realities of life,

and after a career of immense usefulness as philanthropist and philosopher, died the death of the saint,
honoured by the entire Christian world as the greatest
of the Fathers of the Church.   The life of Addison
furnishes another such example.   He, who was known
in after-life as a bashful, taciturn man, whose lips were
sealed on the appearance of a single stranger, was,
while at school, up to any 'lark,' and was once even
a ringleader in a barring out.   Boys will be boys,
after all, and most men are the better for having been
boys at one time of their life.   Malabari, as we have
said, was a boy in the full sense of the word, and
extracted the utmost enjoyment out of this, on the
whole, happy period of life.   But in his wildest boyish
mood we find nothing cruelly wanton; on the contrary,
in several of the stories he has related of his early
days in his delightful autobiographic sketches, we
already trace his generosity and tenderness of heart,
ever ready to befriend a fellow-being, man, woman or
child, in trouble; and even, if need be, to bring trouble
upon himself in the act.   But the terrible calamity
of his mother's death suddenly and for ever dissipated
his boyish dreams, and transported him into a totally
different and higher sphere.   He becomes, as we have
seen, 'a man at twelve,' left without means and friends.
Hitherto his mother had been to him 'a mighty oak,
under whose boughs' he had rested secure; but
henceforward he had to endure

> 'Sunshine and rain as he might,
> Bare, unshaded, alone,
> Lacking the shelter of her.'
>   MATTHEW ARNOLD, *Rugby Chapel.*

This protection, this shadow was gone, leaving the boy behind an orphan at twelve. The playful roisterer, who had hitherto moved in his little paradise of boyish fun and frolic, was rudely awakened to the stern reality of existence which now presented itself to him, an aspect shorn of all the early romance. The necessity of self-support and self-vigilance, which comes to many later, and to some never, pressed itself upon Malabari very prematurely, though, on the whole, also very wholesomely. The circumstances in which he found himself forced him to discover powers hitherto latent in him. The trial was a severe one, but the boy rose to the occasion and emerged from it quite changed, much the wiser and stronger. The next ten years of his life, from twelve to twenty-two, are the formative period of his character, during which were developed the traits which distinguish his latter years, and by chastening self-discipline were repressed those minor defects which human flesh is heir to, and which so often try to drag down a lofty character. It was the experiences gained in this period that made him what he is, the ever-ready, self-sacrificing champion of human wrong and misery, wherever found, and however deeply and strongly rooted. Born of the people and brought up among them, he now lived in their midst and shared their pleasures and their privations—in short, took a keen human interest in men and their ways. From the touch which he gained with the people even in the lowest ranks of life during those years sprang up the inspiration of his career as an active philan-

thropist and a man of letters. Though a man of
culture in the best sense of this often misapplied word,
he has never allowed his culture to detach him from
the mass of humanity around him and to make him
'live in a world apart,' as has been unfortunately the
case with most so-called cultured men. Though an
ascetic in his habits, having few wants, and these easily
supplied, shrinking from contact with the outer world,
not from a sense of superiority but from an instinctive
dread of publicity, and though in intellect soaring far
above his fellows, genius as he is; yet in feeling he
lives on a level with the lowliest, entering into all
the miseries and sufferings of human life. In this
he is, no doubt, greatly helped by his poetic faculty.
The strong and fertile imagination, which creates for
the poet an ideal world of his own, can also make him
realize much better than ordinary men that hard,
matter-of-fact world around him. Imagination is the
greatest aid to sympathy. One feels best for sufferings
which fall personally under one's own observation and
experience. And the strong imagination, acting in
harmony with a keen sensibility, makes the sufferings
of strangers one's own; the distant in time and space
and relation is made present, and the poet feels for
the woes of a bygone age, for the sufferings of his
contemporaries in the distant land, or for his countrymen with whom he has very little in common, as if
he were feeling for himself and for those most near
and dear to him. Burke, when he prosecuted Warren
Hastings as his bitterest personal enemy, and declaimed
on behalf of the Indian peoples who were separated

from him by half the circumference of the globe,
whom he had never seen and with whom he had
nothing whatever in common, is one of the best
instances on record of such a strong sympathetic
imagination set on fire by the mere reading and
hearing of human wrong. And most active philanthropists derive their first impulse from imagination.
Only the imaginative element has been swamped by
their active philanthropy, and they have left no separate
memorial of their poetic faculty. Malabari has been
more fortunate in this matter, as he has made as deep
a mark on his generation by his poetic effusions as
by his active humane efforts. He has been still more
fortunate in making the two interdependent; he has
made his poetry subserve his philanthropic objects,
and has infused into the latter a good deal of his
poetic genius. His poetry, in fact all his writings,
have a strong human interest about them, which is
quite characteristic of the writer.

For most of this he silently laid the foundation
during the period of his youth, commencing at twelve,
at which tender age, on his mother's death, as we have
seen, he found the world was all before him where to
choose his place of rest. Some natural tears he shed,
but wiped them soon, and manfully set about making
his choice. 'Manfully,' for, as he says, he had actually
become a 'man' at twelve; he began to take views of
life, which persons of twice this age rarely learn to
take :—

> 'A man at twelve, in whom my grief confide?
> No friend to watch me but the sainted guide.
> And when this thought upon my reason stole,

A sudden desolation overspread my soul.
Now sober grown, my mind to study turn'd ;
And thus impell'd, I fresh to school adjourn'd.'

He now longed for knowledge, and looked about for means to obtain it in his destitute condition. The pursuit of knowledge under difficulties is always a congenial theme with biographers, who dwell fondly on the efforts of their young heroes in overcoming obstacles in their path to enlightenment and greatness. We cannot afford to pause here to tell at due length the story of our boy scholar's struggle with adversity, however much we might like to dilate on the subject. Suffice it to say that the battle ended victoriously, as every such battle should end, though, unfortunately, in many instances it does not. Many a rising genius proves unequal to the hard struggle for existence, and is often repressed or crushed ; or, if it survives, lives on in a mutilated, soured condition. Rare are the instances where we see, as in the case of Malabari, the young man emerging from the conflict, not only triumphant, but all the better for having undergone the baptism of fire.

This story is as instructive in the annals of self-help as any to be found in the valuable books of Mr. Smiles or Mr. Craik. Malabari had not entirely wasted his boyhood in rowdy fun. Though not systematically, he had learnt much, and his superiority over his fellows was even then discerned by the more observant. He had no difficulty in finding pupils, some of them older than himself, and by teaching these he was enabled to support as well as educate himself. His mornings and evenings were given to making a small income in this way, while during the intervening hours he attended school. He was now seized by a strong desire to obtain knowledge, and in spite of poverty and want he found means to satisfy it. He was fortunate in joining a good school, and still more so in his Head Master. It was the Irish Presbyterian Mission School, then flourishing at Surat under its excellent head, the Rev. William Dixon, M.A. These mission schools are a distinct feature in the educational system of India, which owes a deep debt to them. Nothing probably impresses on the mind of the people the unselfishness of England in holding and governing India so much as the missionary efforts of the ruling race, and the generous spirit in which they are made. The English missionary is required, by the side of the English civilian and soldier, to give a correct and complete idea of all that the paramount power means to do for the people. It cannot but be touching to find people in a distant land caring so much for the spiritual welfare of their fellow-subjects, and trying to do their best to enlighten, after their own lights, their less favoured brethren; to see the Scotch crofters and Irish peasants, themselves steeped in poverty, contribute voluntarily and cheerfully their hard-earned pennies for the education and conversion of the Indians. The direct results of these missionary efforts, in which not only does each of the three countries of the United Kingdom take its proper share, but to which also the more distant and disinterested country of New England beyond the Atlantic contributes its mite, may not be encouraging;

nay, they may be said to be disappointing. But
indirectly, by the means which they employ of
disseminating knowledge among the masses who
would otherwise remain in ignorance and superstition,
the missionaries are doing great good to the country.
India has attracted the kindly attention of nearly all
Churches and all denominations of Christianity, most
of which have their schools and colleges, to which the
natives flock in even greater number than to similar
institutions under the direct care of Government.
Though they have not yet succeeded in converting
anything like an adequate proportion of their scholars,
the missionaries may take legitimate pride in being so
largely instrumental in bringing about the remarkable
renascence of the Indian intellect, which is now being
witnessed all over the land. The whole country is
parcelled out among the various rival Churches, and
in many of the large towns they are all to be found
working side by side, though not always shoulder to
shoulder.

It was one of these schools that young Malabari
joined at Surat, and where, under very sound and
sympathetic guidance, he began his acquaintance with
the English language, which later developed into
absolute mastery. The Head Master, William Dixon,
was the type of a true missionary, pious and unworldly;
and seeing the work done by his young pupil, he took
very kindly to him and encouraged him in various
ways. He introduced him into his family, a great
privilege for a young man in his position, and brought
him under the beneficial influence of Mrs. Dixon, which

Malabari still remembers gratefully. The exemplary Christian life led by the little household at Surat impressed him deeply, and must be reckoned as the first formative influence on his character during this period. Two diligent years were spent thus, in learning and teaching, and so rapid was his progress that he was fairly ready now to appear for the University Entrance or Matriculation Examination that is held every year at the Presidency town of Bombay. There was the pecuniary difficulty, however, in the way of a journey to Bombay, and of paying the fees, which would have been at once overcome if the shy young man had told Mr. Dixon of it. But he was too shy to ask for anything. Help, however, came from a very unexpected quarter. A Parsi money-lender in the street, who was known to be very close-fisted, hearing of the case, volunteered to help our young genius, and it may be taken for granted that the old gentleman was glad all his life he had done so.

Thus Malabari left Surat and came to Bombay for his examination, intending to return soon after. But circumstances tending otherwise, he has ever since been domiciled in Bombay. The examination proved too stiff in one branch, and he failed to pass it. The test was a severe one, as it included many heterogeneous subjects, demanding a fair knowledge of the English language, itself a very difficult foreign tongue to the Indian youth, and of another so-called classical language, with the elements of history, ancient and modern, geography, political and physical, natural science, including astronomy and chemistry, and mathematics, including arithmetic, algebra, and geometry. This must be a difficult course for any lad of fifteen. But in the case of the Indian the difficulty is enhanced by the fact that knowledge in all these multifarious subjects has to be imparted through the foreign English tongue. The strain thus early put upon the young mind at the threshold of the University is continued in an aggravated form during its career therein; it is stuffed with a bewildering diversity of subjects at high pressure, to the detriment of originality and sound judgement. This heavy mental strain re-acts on the body, and the naturally weak constitution of the Indian youth, who has to pursue his studies under circumstances widely different from those of his brother in Europe, without physical exercise and healthy social relaxation, is soon undermined, physical and mental decay often prematurely sets in, and many promising careers are cut short in the early prime of life. Many instances of such premature and rapid deaths among young University men have only recently occurred, and have set the public pondering seriously over the causes of this melancholy result. But there are many more such men, who, though alive, have belied the promise of their early youth, owing to the premature decay of mental and physical vitality, brought about by an unnatural and, in some respects, false system of education.

Malabari fortunately escaped the rigours of this system. Though his aspirations after an academic career were very high and intense at first, he had to yield to circumstances, and give up all hopes of entering college. The entrance test, as we have said, was too severe for him in one branch, that of mathematics, though in all other subjects, especially in English, he did very well. The youthful ardour of our aspirant after University honours was thus damped in the very beginning, and he must return to Surat, to his pupils and his school. But a friend to whom he was introduced thought he could as well have pupils in Bombay as at Surat, and introduced him in his turn to the Head Master of a large Parsi High School, who at once saw that there was more in the shy young man than met the eye. Pupils were readily found for him, and an adequate income was assured. He now earned his livelihood in ease and in a congenial manner; he had, moreover, leisure left for satisfying his own thirst for knowledge and for literary pursuits.

He cultivated his natural bent for literature, especially poetry, and ranged, in a desultory manner, over a wide field of English verse. His mastery over the language was increasing, and it is interesting to find him appreciating rationally and critically, even at that early age, most of the greatest poets of England. 'I have ranged aimlessly,' says he, 'over a very wide field of poetry, English as well as Indian ; also Persian and Greek translated. As to English masters, Shakespeare was my daily companion during school days, and a long while after that. Much of my worldly knowledge I owe to this greatest of seers and practical thinkers. Milton filled me with awe. Somehow, I used to feel unhappy when the turn came for *Paradise Lost.* His torrents of words frightened me as much by their stateliness as by monotony.   Nor could I sympathize with some of the personal teachings of this grand old singer. (Wordsworth is my philosopher, Tennyson my poet.) Amongst my many prizes at school I remember having received a bulky volume, named *Selections from British Poets*, carried home for me by an older companion.   I used to dip into this unwieldy folio, and got to know a little of Chaucer, Spenser, and other stars, earlier as well as later, through it.   At school I had Campbell for another favourite, preferred Dryden to Pope, and Scott to several of his contemporaries.   Cowper and Goldsmith I have always valued as dear old schoolmasters, Byron and Burns are boon companions when in the mood ; Shelley and Keats as explorers of dreamland, who fascinate one by their subtle fancies.

CHAPTER III.

FROM reading and admiring poetry to writing it was
but one step, and that was soon taken. Indeed, many
of his poems were written very early, when a mere
schoolboy, and his first appearance before the public
was as a poet. But it was not as a poet in the foreign
English language just yet. It was his mother-tongue
that claimed him first as a poet. And it is his mother-
tongue, too, that has welcomed the latest offspring of
his muse, as may be seen from his little volume of
poems, entitled *Experiences of Life*, which he has
lately published. Born in the very heart of Gujarat,
and bred in one of its chief cities amid Gujarati
surroundings, Malabari has a great affection for the
Gujarati language, in which he lisped out his first
thoughts, in which he heard those songs of the
minstrels, which, as we have seen, had such a fascination for him in his restless early days, whose poetical
literature, such as it was, he cultivated with fond
affection, and which was hallowed to him by many
grateful associations.

In this love for his vernacular language, which he
has practically shown by enriching its literature with

several volumes, considered as standard works by competent judges, Malabari stands almost alone among his cultured contemporaries. With the spread of a knowledge of the English language and the splendid literature, not of England alone, but of the whole civilized world, ancient and modern, embodied in it, the old languages of India are naturally losing ground among the newly-educated classes. These, being introduced to the far richer language of their rulers, and perceiving its many great advantages, are exhausting their efforts in obtaining a mastery over it. Among its most important advantages, they have found that it can supply the outward uniting bond to the peoples of the various provinces, and thus aid them in giving vent to their present political aspirations.

India being a vast continent, and its different provinces being in reality separate countries, like those of Europe, differing from one another in race, religion, and climate, it has no common language, which is the very first, though not the only condition of nationality. It has a score of vernaculars, spoken in its various parts, and quite unintelligible and foreign to one another. The Bengali spoken in the northeast, and the Marathi spoken in the west, differ as much from each other and from the Tamil spoken in the south and the Hindi in the north, as Spanish differs from Russian. The newly-educated classes, with strong political aspirations, observing this drawback to mutual intercourse, are rapidly making the English language their common medium of communication, whereby the barriers created by the vernaculars are thrown down.

The rulers' tongue is rapidly becoming the uniting bond of thought and speech to the heterogeneous mass of educated youths throughout the continent. This is in itself a proud achievement, and it must be very gratifying to an Englishman to contemplate that his language has gone forth, out of its own small island home, to the far East, and is working there a marvellous revolution. This triumph is the greater, because India is no new country, wanting a language and literature ; but one in reality having languages which were perfected before English began to be uttered by human lips, and it contains poetical and philosophical literature of a very high order.

But what has been the gain of the foreign language has proved the ruin of the indigenous tongues. Our educated men vie with one another in acquiring a mastery of the former, and neglect the latter as useless. The vernaculars are being everywhere supplanted, even in every-day intercourse, among the younger generation. The best talents being drawn towards the much more attractive language of the rulers, the vernaculars have to languish in the hands of in-competent writers without culture. It might have been expected that when first the native Indian mind was brought into contact with the English language and its literature, it would improve and invigorate its own indigenous languages by this wholesome contact, and infuse into them new strength derived from the foreigner. What happened to the English language itself in the fifteenth and sixteenth centuries, when English scholars were largely introduced to the classical

languages and literatures of Greece and Rome, might
also have fallen to the lot of the Indian vernaculars ; and they too would have become more elastic
and robust, with a more varied and wealthy literature.
Instead of neglecting, almost abandoning their own,
the Indian youths might improve them by adapting
and ingrafting what they find best in the new.   Perhaps
a later generation may do that.   So far, however, it has
not been done, and it may be said that the rising
talents of the country are doing very little to cultivate
their mother-tongues and so enrich their literatures.
This is really crippling their own usefulness.   The
English educated class must, in the very nature of
things, be a very small minority, and it can hope to
influence the great mass of its countrymen only
through their own indigenous languages.   An English
speech or an English book by an educated Indian can
only be meant for the eyes and ears of the rulers, or
for the small band of his educated fellows.   It cannot
reach the overwhelming majority of the people, whom
it should be the chief aim of the educated minority to
influence and improve with the aid of the superior
light which they have seen.   A command over the
vernaculars, if wielded by men who have also had
access to Western learning, would have the greatest
influence over the people in India.

This power it has been the good fortune of very
few to wield.   In the west of India Malabari is one of
the very few who possess it.   He alone may be said
to have excelled in both the foreign language as well
as his own vernacular, and enriched each with the best

things, derived from the other. The reproach, to
which most of our English educated men are liable,
of allowing their mother-tongues to languish, and
neglecting so far the interests of their uneducated
countrymen, cannot apply to him. He has from the
first used his mother-tongue to address himself to his
own people. His poetical genius finds congenial vent
in Gujarati, and through his poems he has successfully sought to impart, in a pleasing channel, much
that is best in Western culture, combined with the
excellences of indigenous thought and language.
Malabari is a born poet, and it may be with truth
said of him that he 'lisped in numbers, for the numbers came' to him. Many of his poems, published
later, were jotted down in early boyhood, in happy
moments of inspiration, and many more must have
perished unwritten and unrecorded. When he took
passionately to study and self-culture he polished some
of these early effusions, added to them others, and
made up the whole into a little volume. This was
the sole capital that he brought with him to Bombay
from Surat, at the age of fifteen, much as Johnson
came to London from his native town of Lichfield
with his life of Savage and the tragedy of Irene in
his pocket. The manuscript was fated to be neglected
for some time yet, ere it could see the light of day.
But before that it proved signally useful to him in an
unexpected way. It became the means of bringing him
out of his obscurity, and of his being introduced to a
man who exercised great influence at a critical time on
his life and character.

In a happy moment Malabari resolved to take his little manuscript of Gujarati verse to the Rev. J. Van Somern Taylor, who was one of his examiners, and well known for his mastery over the Gujarati language. The missionaries have recognized the great importance of learning the vernaculars of the provinces in which they have to work, as they have to deal with the ignorant masses of the population. Hence their attitude towards these languages has been quite the opposite of that of the educated natives. It is a very fortunate thing for the vernaculars that cultured Europeans leave their homes and settle in the country, devoting their best efforts to cultivating these vernaculars assiduously. Some of the best books recently published in the languages are by such scholarly missionaries, who have produced excellent dictionaries, grammars, and other useful works. Mr. Taylor had devoted himself to the Gujarati language, which he laid under lasting obligation by writing its standard grammar, based on principles of philology. His acquaintance with Gujarati literature was accurate and wide, and his scholarship was critical, owing to his knowledge of European methods.

Mr. Taylor was very agreeably surprised at the high order of merit evinced by the Parsi stranger's verses, and became deeply interested in his discovery. A new genius was before him, he felt sure, and he tried to help him to rise. With this object, he introduced him to one who could help the boy effectively. This was the famous Scotch missionary, Dr. John Wilson, who was then nearing the end of his long career of varied public usefulness and private virtues.) He had come out as a young man in the early part of the century to Bombay, and domiciling himself there, and devoting his rare abilities to doing practical good to its peoples, had exercised a most beneficial influence over two generations of its life. As scholar, educationist, controversialist, active philanthropist and zealous missionary, and, above all, as a man of rare public and private virtues, he made a mark on his times. For nearly half a century he was the moving spirit and leader of society in Bombay, and during this whole period he enjoyed the respect and esteem of the various rival communities which make up the life of the Western Presidency of India. Though he had come out from his native country only as a missionary, to preach the Gospel according to the lights of his own denomination to the peoples of Western India, he took a wider and more liberal view of his duties, and laboured hard in doing good to the people, spiritually and mentally, in every way he could. Every scheme of public beneficence found in him a ready and steady supporter, regardless of creed or colour. His efforts for the suppression of female infanticide in Kathiawad and elsewhere, on which subject he wrote a useful and exhaustive work, attest his practical disinterested philanthropy, as he could not hope for the conversion of those whom he was instrumental in saving from a cruel death, inflicted by the same parental hands which nature had provided for their protection. He cultivated nearly every language, modern and classical, of the peoples with whom he had to deal, and obtained a mastery over them which enabled him to publish several important works, highly valued by Indian scholars themselves.   He was one of the earliest English scholars to study the Zend and Pahlavi languages, in which the fragments of the sacred books of the Parsis are preserved, and his book on this religion is the first which shows acquaintance with these writings at first hand.   His labours on the cave temples of Western India, and his other archaeological studies, showed literary zeal and ability which alone would have sufficed to make him famous. As an educationist, he did probably the greatest good. He presided over the birth of European education in the country, and followed it throughout his career with anxious and watchful care, aiding the Government in its efforts, as well as working independently with his chosen band of devoted followers.   He founded schools in various towns, which disseminated primary education among the poorest, whom he took specially under his charge; while the college which now bears his honoured name was founded and conducted by him to impart to young Indians the highest secular and religious knowledge of the West.   The Bombay University, with which he was connected from its very foundation in 1858, and of which he was for a long time the unofficial head as Vice-Chancellor, received the benefit of his wide experience gained in Europe as well as in India, and was guided during the period of its infancy by his wise counsels.

But amidst his various self-imposed duties, Dr. Wilson never forgot that his principal duty was to disseminate

the Word of God and to confute what appeared to
him to be the pernicious errors of Oriental heathen-
dom. His whole life was dominated by this purpose
to which all others were subordinated. His learning
and scholarship, his dialectical ability, his active philanthropy were all dedicated to the service of God and
furthering the knowledge of His Word. He entered
into religious controversies with the prevailing Indian
sects, doubtless at first with the disinterested object of
exposing their errors and the hope of convincing his
opponents. But his zeal sometimes outran the bounds
of prudence and, it must be added with regret, of
charity. Unnecessary personal bitterness was at times
created, which, instead of bringing Christianity nearer
to the Indian mind, tended to widen the breach and
retard the approach of reconciliation.

An instance of this was his famous controversy with
the Parsis, which was carried on with perhaps needless
acerbity on both sides, and of which ill-feeling was for
some time the chief result. These descendants of the
ancient Persians and the inheritors of the noble tradi-
tions of Xerxes and Darius, and of the still nobler
faith of the Prophet of Bactria, had found, after
numerous vicissitudes on the fall of their power in
their native country, and the ruin of their religion at
the hands of persecuting Islam in the seventh century,
a peaceful asylum on the Western coast of India under
the Hindus. For centuries, under the Hindu and the
Mahomedan rule, they just managed to exist as
a separate body, with a faith as well as most of the
manners and customs of their own, without merging

into the overwhelmingly large communities surrounding them.   But under the fostering care of the British
they soon found opportunities to develop their ancient
virtues, and became in a short time the leading community among the natives, owing to their excellent
business qualities, enterprising spirit, quickness of perception, and ready adaptability.   They have been the
first to benefit by the English rule in India, and in
their turn they try to transmit these benefits to the
people around them.   By their natural ability and
position in the country they were well fitted thus to
be the mediators between the rulers and the ruled ;
and they are now playing this part to a considerable
extent.   In political and literary matters the Parsis
have led the Hindus and the Mahomedans.   At the
head of most political associations, at any rate in
Bombay, and in the vanguard of those who fight.
rightly or wrongly, for the political advancement of
educated Indians, are to be found men of this race.
It is a Parsi for whom has been reserved the unique
position of being the first Oriental to take a seat in
the British House of Commons.   In physical matters,
too, Parsis are rapidly evolving robuster qualities of
body, which will in the long run make them the equals
of many Western nations, and on which Western
supremacy mainly rests.   In social matters they easily
take the lead of their Hindu countrymen, as they are
singularly free from those narrow views of caste which
hamper the latter.   As we shall see, it is a Parsi, the
subject of our theme, who has taken up the cause of
social reform among the Hindu population, and tried

to better the lot of millions of women, mute victims of unequal laws and customs manufactured during the dark ages of Indian history.

The Parsis have thus been the most prominent community among the natives: it is scarcely possible to conceive of the public life of Western India without them. They have, therefore, attracted the attention of Europeans to an extent commensurate with their abilities and importance. Christian missionaries have sought them specially, and have tried hard to spread the Christian faith among them, with the hope of influencing the other Indian communities through the Parsis. From the early days of proselytizing efforts to our own, Parsis have been the object of great solicitude to European missions. But the men who had given up all their early possessions, and left their native country itself, to launch on unknown seas in order to seek a new home for their ancient faith—men who, though a mere handful, preserved their race and religion intact during twelve stormy centuries in the country of their adoption—were scarcely the stuff of which proselytes are made. Those who had resisted the destructive persecuting force of Islam, were not likely to yield to the mild arguments of Christian missionaries. Most efforts to convert them have proved fruitless. Beyond stray individual cases of conversion, Christianity seems to have failed to make way among this intelligent and liberal-minded community.

Dr. Wilson realized the importance of converting the Parsis at the very beginning of his career in Bombay, and he at once set about the task. He preached eloquent sermons, wrote learned treatises, held conferences, brought his personal influence to bear on individuals. But most of this to little purpose. His first great campaign against their religion lasted for twelve years, during which he exhausted all his efforts and underwent great sacrifices in order to gain his disinterested object. But the result was disappointing. The conversion of a few school-boys was the net gain; whilst the whole community was made more hostile than ever to the faith which was sought to be thrust upon them, and actively resented the zeal of the missionaries. Even after this failure, Dr. Wilson never lost heart, and availed himself of every opportunity to bring the Parsis to the fold of Christ. But these attempts tended to exasperate the people. To judge from the literature to which these efforts gave rise among the Parsis, their irritation must have been unlimited, as they attacked the foundation of all religions in fighting against Christianity, and employed the arguments of deists like Voltaire and Tom Paine, whose works they translated into their vernacular. Who can tell how much of the atheism and indifference to all religion, which is to be seen among the Parsis at the present day, is due to the reaction caused in the last generation by the undoubtedly well-meant but indiscreet efforts of the missionaries?

But whatever may be said of his injudicious zeal, Dr. Wilson's motive was thoroughly disinterested. If he had depended on his personal influence, instead of launching into polemics, he would have been probably more successful. For those who were unmoved

by his logic, however faultless, would relent as soon
as they were brought face to face with his sweet personal life. In his controversies he sometimes did
great injustice to his heart which overflowed with
charity and goodwill to all. His door was open to ·
every one in distress, and no one sought his help in
vain. Many a time he was deceived by designing
persons, but he never allowed such untoward occur-
rences to stand in the way of relieving distress. There
must be many persons, still alive, who owe their start
in life and worldly position to the friendly help of this
magnanimous Christian missionary. He had come to
possess influence in the highest quarters, and he used
it all disinterestedly. He took a special interest in
rising talent. And many a struggling young man of
promise was rescued by him, and put on the path to
success.

It was to such a man that Mr. Taylor introduced
young Malabari, at just the time of life to be benefited by contact with a strong and righteous personality. The aged philanthropist was himself struck
by the young Parsi, and took him under his special
charge. He soon arranged to have the little volume
of verse published, after obtaining for it the support
it so richly deserved. He introduced the author to
several influential citizens, who helped him not a little
in his onward career. It may be here mentioned that
Malabari has been fortunate in some of his friends,
who took him by the hand at the right time. So far
we have seen that on critical occasions friends came
forward almost providentially to assist him. Later he

had much more powerful friends who were willing to
ensure his worldly success.   But his unselfishness appears nowhere more clear and convincing than in his
refusal to aggrandize himself through his friends and
connexions.   A man in the position which he came to
occupy must have possessed self-control of no ordinary
kind to have resisted temptations to which most men
yield.

Wilson brought his young scholar to the notice of
the munificent Parsi knight, Sir Cawasji Jehangier,
whose charities are well known in England as well as
India.   Sir Cawasji seems to have taken very kindly to
his young friend.   He introduced him to Mr. Martin
Wood, then editor of the *Times of India*, who, a little
later, utilized his talents in the field of journalism,
and trained him to that noble profession of which
Malabari is now the chief ornament among his countrymen.   Dr. Wilson, as we have seen, arranged for the
printing of the little volume of Gujarati verse, obtaining for it the support of the Government and of
a few wealthy citizens ; and the book appeared in 1875
after some delay caused by the author's ignorance of
business matters.

It was named by its patron *Niti-Vinod*, or the
Pleasures of Morality.   The title is misleading in
one way, as it recalls analogous poems in English
with similar titles, like Campbell's *Pleasures of Hope*,
Akenside's *Pleasures of the Imagination*, and Rogers'
Pleasures of Memory.   *Niti-Vinod* is not one con-
tinuous poem, like these, with a fixed theme, but
a collection of short poems of very unequal merit, the

best of which are lyrical. The title is justified chiefly by the strong moral tone which pervades the whole, and which, in fact, is the chief characteristic of the writer. Moral earnestness and a strong faith in the eternal and universal law of right and wrong are the characteristics of the poems and the poet.

The book is divided into five parts, treating of moral and religious subjects, metaphysical and social problems, miscellaneous questions of interest and brief sketches of the lives of local and other celebrities that seem to have fired the writer's enthusiasm. The lines preaching devotion and detachment from the world are specially noteworthy, written as they were by a poet as yet in his teens. In the range of Gujarati literature it would be difficult to find a poet who, at twice or three times Malabari's age, could display his spiritual insight and wisdom. Some of these early efforts are equally noteworthy in that we find in them the first signs of the author's intense sympathy with the child-wives and girl-widows of India. The poems dealing with these subjects are very pathetic, proceeding from the depth of his heart. How he translated his thoughts and feelings into action, and materially helped to alleviate the sufferings which he here deplores, we shall see in the proper place.

The poems were written in his own vernacular, which is the language of Gujarat. But this Gujarati language has split itself almost into two dialects, owing to the two races that use it, the Hindus and the Parsis. It is derived from the parent stock of the Sanskrit, the classical language of ancient India, as much as French and the other Romance languages of Southern Europe are derived from the Latin in the middle ages. The Hindus try to preserve and develop this original Sanskrit element, and guard it jealously against any foreign intrusion. In their vocabulary and grammar they try as much as possible to keep close to the classical model. The Parsis, on the other hand, who have by the necessity of the case to use the language of the province in which they have settled for so long, have tried to keep down the Sanskrit element. They have no such fond regard for that ancient language as the Hindus have ; Sanskrit is not hallowed to them by glorious associations of old as in the eyes of these latter. Their ancient language is Persian, connected through Pazand and Pahlavi with the Zend or Avesta, the language in which their oldest sacred books are written. Their study of Persian has led them to introduce largely the Persian element into their Gujarati vernacular, and to eschew as much as possible the Sanskrit. Latterly, the great zest with which they have taken to the English language has also made them introduce an English element into it ; English words are either taken up bodily or slightly modified ; the structure of sentences is modelled after the English ; while English modes of expression and composition are finding almost universal favour among them. The result has been that there are two kinds of Gujarati, the Hindu and the Parsi Gujarati, which, in course of time, may become two distinct dialects almost unintelligible to each other. —

The tendency at present is for the two to separate more widely. Hindu writers are becoming purists, and drawing more and more upon the Sanskrit, even for things which that language is not capable of supplying. With their peculiar notions they look down upon Parsi Gujarati, and blame the Parsis for defiling their language with foreign mixture. It is getting harder every day for the latter to understand works written by Hindu scholars in their highly Sanskritized Gujarati. The Parsis pursue their own course, diluting the language freely with Persian and English words and idioms, introducing foreign words and constructions, which makes the purists stare and gasp. Both communities are equally active in literature. Both conduct journals in their peculiar Gujarati, write pamphlets, plays and poems. The breach is thus widening. Already English missionaries to Gujarat have seen the necessity of having the Bible translated into both Hindu and Parsi Gujarati, in order to appeal to both separately and effectively.

Malabari's *Niti-Vinod* was written in Hindu Gujarati. Though a Parsi, he has cultivated Hindu Gujarati and its literature with rare success. Classical Gujarati poets like Parmánand, Akha, Narsi Mehta, Dayaram and others, he seems to have read with some attention; and the itinerant minstrels, as we have seen, had a sensible influence on him in his early Surat days. The ethical tone of his poetry springs, of course, from his own intense moral earnestness. But no small part of it could be traced to his acquaintance with some of these poets and minstrels. The bards and minstrels revelled in a bewildering variety of metres, and their young admirer followed them closely in this respect, as may be seen from numerous pieces in this book, which gives a good idea of the metric resources of the language.

From its peculiar character the Gujarati language is very well adapted to singing; better, it is claimed, than English. The various metres, if well handled, have a pleasing lyrical effect. To be appreciated properly, they must be sung. Many pieces in the *Niti-Vinod* have already become popular songs among Hindus of Gujarat, and the effect of the poet's high moral tone and lofty standard of life on the people, must prove beneficial. Genuine poets among them are very rare in these days. Not a few of their best poets follow a questionable standard. of ethics. The advent of a poet, then, who combined the lyrical excellence of the indigenous singers with the lofty moral tone, partly inherited and partly acquired from his intimacy with the best poetical literature of his own people as well as of Europe, could not but be hailed as a blessing. The poems were very favourably received on almost all hands.

The unusual thing about them was that they were liked by both Hindus and Parsis. The Parsis were proud that one of themselves had successfully shown to the Hindus that they too were able to wield their language. Their newspapers praised the writer's skill in the use of the Sanskrit Gujarati and its various metres. One of the leading papers among these recognized him as 'the first genuine poet among the

Parsis,' who had expressed his sentiments in pure Gujarati and in sweet and beautiful verse. The Hindus were surprised to find such a mastery over their language as they found in the new volume, and their first living poets hastened to welcome this new-comer to their ranks. One of these expressed his opinion that 'such wide acquaintance with Gujarati, such beauty of versification, and such a delightful combination of sentiment and imagination would do honour to the pen of any accomplished Hindu poet.' Another, who was considered the laureate of Gujarat, and whose poems are the delight of every Hindu household in the province, wrote, 'it is a general belief amongst us that Parsis cannot excel in versification through the medium of correct and idiomatic Gujarati ; but Mr. Malabari's *Niti-Vinod* effectually dispels that belief.' An English critic regarded the book rightly as an attempt 'to infuse into the Eastern mind some-thing of the lofty tone of thought and feeling which distinguishes the most approved literary productions of the West,' and gave due praise to the author's 'wonderful command over the pure Hindu Gujarati.'

CHAPTER IV.

WITH this volume, containing the first-fruits of his poetic genius, unequal and irregular though the verses were, Malabari emerged from obscurity, and began to be known beyond the small circle of his personal friends. His means, too, were increasing. The talented tutor was well spoken of on all sides, and pupils flocked to him. He soon found himself in a position to marry and become a family man. Of his married life this only need be said here, that it has been a happy one as regards mutual affection and esteem, and that in the wife the husband has found exactly what he himself lacks, namely, order and economy. This he often gratefully acknowledges as a gift from Providence. In the matter of marriage the life of the educated Indian of to-day has many and serious drawbacks. If he finds in his wife a loving partner of his worldly fortunes, a good manager of his domestic affairs and trainer of his children, he should consider himself happy. It is all that an Indian wife could be expected to prove herself. But if he seeks for an intelligent companion, on anything like terms of equality, with intellectual sympathy for his hopes and aspirations, a helpmate in his affairs beyond those of the household, he is in most cases doomed to disappointment. His life is in this way seriously handicapped, as compared with that of the European, next to whom stands the Parsi. As often as not, the Indian wife, instead of being a helpmate in his pursuits, and sympathizing with his aims and aspirations, is a hindrance, a veritable thorn in his side, standing up for obsolete and exploded superstitions, dragging her partner down with her. The utmost that he can pray for, in such a case, is apathy. It is not difficult to explain the cause of this deplorable state of things. Female education has been almost entirely neglected in India up till quite recently. The aims of life and conduct of the younger generation have been revolutionized by the new learning to which they have been introduced. Lofty ideals and high hopes, however selfish these may be in some cases, are cherished as a rule by our young men far above the level of former generations. But the female mind has remained almost · entirely where it was, moving in the same narrow grooves. Very little effort has been made to get the new light to reach the women. Hence English educated Indians have to rest content with more or less ignorant and unsympathetic partners in life. They are beginning to perceive the mischief; and an honest attempt is now being made to educate Hindu girls to something at least approaching the standard of the education of boys. But deep-rooted prejudices have to be overcome. The dogma of the absolute inferiority of woman in every respect to man prevails in the country with irresistible force, and it will take long to weaken it so far as to allow the despised female to have the same share of education and the same sphere of action as the male.

The Parsis, the community to which Malabari belongs, saw the necessity of educating their girls much earlier than the Hindus and the Mahomedans, to whom they may be said to have shown the way in this, as in most other respects. Still, though the great proportion of their young women are not so illiterate as among others, educated Parsi youths cannot be said to be much better off in married life than their Hindu and Mahomedan fellows. There are instances of what we may call equal marriages, wherein the couples are well mated with regard to intellectual sympathy. But in the generality of cases, even among Parsis, the wife is little more than a physical companion, sharing no more of her husband's aspirations than those of a stranger. The life of the educated Indian is much to be pitied on this account. Foreigners cannot conceive what a drag such unions often are on our public men. Great, therefore, must be the credit given to those who rise superior to the difficulties of the situation, and though not on the same level, compete as if on equal terms with European workers and come so close to them in the race of public usefulness. Malabari, as we have seen, is happy in his married life, with an affectionate wife and loving children. But in his case, too, as in that of most public men of modern India, it must be admitted that his family cannot be of much direct help to him in his public career by sharing and lightening its burdens.

After his first failure to pass the matriculation examination, Malabari did not give up hope, but persevered steadily for three successive years, and at length succeeded in 1871 in passing that difficult test. He overcame his 'aversion to arithmetic, the subject that had stood cruelly in his way and rendered nugatory the excellent results in English and other branches. But he did not continue his studies after passing the entrance test, and never entered college. This was perhaps as well. Though he failed to receive what is called an academic training, and has not the honour to be a graduate of the University, he excels most of his contemporaries with the best collegiate education at their back, in literary ability, grace of diction, and more especially, in originality. This last quality would most likely have suffered if he had been put through the treadmill of the University curriculum at present in vogue.

The University has been fairly successful in producing good professional men, lawyers, doctors, engineers; and above all, in furnishing to Government a useful and reliable body of subordinate officials in the Civil Service, through whom the work of administration is in a great measure carried on. But its success is doubtful as regards rearing up a body of really cultured men, deep thinkers and great writers. Indian Universities have existed for more than a generation, and their roll of graduates is long. But among these will be found very few who have made a deep mark on their times as writers, thinkers, or great characters.   On the contrary, such great forces are to be found outside their pale : men like Keshub Chunder Sen in Bengal and Malabari in Bombay owe little to academic education.   This failure, so far, of the Universities, upon which high hopes were based by the Government and the people, is now attracting a good deal of attention. Too much thought cannot be given to the subject by those who have the future welfare of the country at heart.

The year after the publication of his Gujarati poems, our author appeared in the more ambitious rôle of a poet in the foreign English language. We have seen how passionately he took to the study of some of the English poets.   With his poetical temperament he entered into the very spirit of these masters, discovered hidden affinities, and assimilated much that was best in them.   Almost with the commencement of his study of the English poets he took to composing verses in English, and some of these he had written already as a boy at Surat.   Many of them seem to have suggested themselves to him while reading his favourite pieces on which they are modelled.   The command over the language, which they show, is truly astonishing in a youth under twenty.   These verses he showed to his friend and benefactor, Dr. Wilson, who thought that they displayed 'an uncommonly intimate knowledge of the English language' and were 'the outcome of a gifted mind, trained to habits of deep meditation and fresh and felicitous expression.' Meeting with such kindly encouragement, Malabari

polished his early effusions, added new ones, and made
up the whole into a thin octavo volume of just
a hundred pages. It was given the appropriate title
of the *Indian Muse in English Garb,* and was dedicated in a graceful letter to Miss Mary Carpenter,
a lady who had been working at great sacrifice,
steadily and long, for the cause which the poet was
himself soon to take up, that of the helpless women
of India.

Malabari was twenty-three when this thin little
volume appeared. It was his first appearance in
public in a most difficult foreign language, and argued
rare courage in challenging the judgement of the literary
world at the commencement of his career. Though
some few Indians had attempted English verse before
him, yet this volume was perhaps the first of its kind
to arrest attention both in India and in England. The
newspapers on the whole welcomed our youthful poet
heartily. He received still more cordial encouragement from some of the leading literary men of the time
in England to whom copies had been sent. (Tennyson
wrote to him to say 'it is interesting, and more than
interesting, to see how well you have managed in the
English garb.') He expressed a wish to be able to read
the poems Malabari had written in his own vernacular,
and signed himself 'Your far-away but sincere friend.'
Lord Shaftesbury, John Bright, and other prominent
men also praised the sentiments and the style of the
verses.

Professor Max Müller, with whom the poet was
to come in closer contact later, and whom he has

impressed deeply enough to be reckoned among the select circle of half a dozen of his intimate Indian friends, showed great discrimination in the remark that 'it is in the verses where you feel and speak like a true Indian that you seem to me to speak most like a true poet.' Being himself a foreigner to the English language, who had succeeded in obtaining a wonderful mastery over it, he could appreciate the difficulties of the Indian aspirant to literary fame as well as give him sound advice. ('To me also,' wrote he, 'English is an acquired language, but I have never attempted more than English prose. However, whether we write English verse or English prose, let us never forget that the best service we can render is to express our truest Indian or German thoughts in English, and thus to act as honest interpreters between nations that ought to understand each other much better than they do at present. Depend upon it, the English public, at least the better part of it, like a man who is what he is. The very secret of the excellence of English literature lies in the independence, the originality, and truthfulness of English writers.') Miss Florence Nightingale also welcomed the *Indian Muse* in an enthusiastic letter to the poet, which ended in these inspiriting words : 'May God bless your labours! May the Eternal Father bless India, bless England, and bring us together as one family, doing each other good ! May the fire of His love, the sunshine of His countenance, inspire us all !'

The contents of the *Indian Muse* are miscellaneous, many of them being occasional pieces suggested by

men and events of the time in Western India, such as
the career of the then recently deposed Gaikwad of
Baroda, and the visit of the Prince of Wales to Bombay
in 1875. There are, also, some characteristic poems in
the volume; the autobiographic sketch, from which we
have already quoted, belongs to this volume. The
death of his friend, Dr. Wilson—'the friend of my
youth'—forms the subject of a pathetic poem 'To the
memory of one of the noblest friends of India.' The
miseries of Hindu female life are vividly depicted in
the person of an orphan girl-widow who is made to
tell her own heartrending story. The lines on the
'British character,' and to the 'Disloyal Grumbler,'
reveal his political views. His deep sympathy with
the people of India, his admiration for the work of the
English Government and his appreciation of their
sterling qualities, as also of the enormous difficulties of
the administration of a foreign country—views to which
he has clung in the main—have made him a force in
public affairs, an accredited interpreter between the
rulers and the ruled. Some lines from the address to
the 'Disloyal Grumbler' are well worth quoting at the
present day, as they strike the keynote, thus early, of
the politics of our patriot-poet and those who think
with him :—

> 'O mourn thou not in vain regrets
> That fancied wrong thy peace alloys;
> When thy ungrateful heart forgets
> What bliss thy conquered race enjoys
> What if thy English brother lords
> It o'er thee, with contempt implied?
> Recall the day when Moslem swords
> Cut thee and thine in wanton pride!

> Think how a gen'rous nation strives
> To win thee back thy prestige lost;
> Of what dear joys herself deprives,
> To aid thee at a frightful cost.'

Then, after describing, in eloquent verse, the sacrifice made by Britain for the cause of good government in India, he proceeds :—

> 'When thoughts of this my senses crowd,
> Good God! my nerves are all unstrung;
> Hot tears of shame my vision shroud,
> Hot tears by grateful pity wrung.
> And none, with common souls with mine,
> But feels his patriot's sense profaned
> If, yielding to the morbid whine,
> One prates of rights and powers restrained.
> From motives int'rested apart,
> As guardian of our peace and pride,
> In every honest British heart,
> I hail my brother, friend and guide!
> And tho' my heart, my head, my hand,
> My country's welfare holds in pawn,
> Still more I owe to that brave land,
> From which alone that welfare's drawn.

The admirable good sense of these lines strikes one more forcibly when he remembers that they were penned by an Indian poet, hardly out of his teens. Let us not forget, also, that the career of the full-grown man has faithfully followed the note struck here in his boyish days. Love and admiration of all that is best in English life and character is, indeed, the pervading characteristic of the poetry as of the author's mind and heart. It is not indiscriminate rhapsody in which he indulges. He has entered into the very spirit of English thought and action, having penetrated the outer crust which repels most Indian thinkers from them. His lines to the 'Genius of the Bard of Rydal' show that Malabari could take a correct measure, even at this early age, of the influence on England of one of her greatest masters. The East is ever present to his mind, and the West is drawn upon, as it were, to make him understand the East the better. Wordsworth reminds him of the venerated founder of his own religion :—

> 'To me, sweet Bard, thy page rare light dictates,
> As on my soul thy magic verse vibrates.
> Thy power seems, in every subtle shade,
> A later offspring of sage Zoroaster's head.
> 'Tween him and thee a common soul I trace
> The same vast genius, but in time and place.
> The same wise judgement in a modest word,
> In one like line the same deep truth unheard.
> The same life's views, the same Heav'n-seeking aim,
> The same your taste, your work and worth the same ;
> Of each, with equal awe, I trembling sing—
> Each mighty mind as Nature's heir and king.'

By the time this first volume of English verse appeared, Malabari's guide, philosopher, and friend was no more. Dr. Wilson closed his long career at the end of 1875 amid unfeigned and universal sorrow. He had dedicated his life to India, and spent it to the very end in its service. To the last his interest in public affairs, and still more in talented individuals among the natives, remained most active. A very short time before his death he was looking forward to introducing the Prince of Wales, who was coming to Bombay, to the antiquities and archaeological curiosities of Western India, of which he was the most zealous and laborious student then alive. But before that opportunity, though so near, could come, Dr. Wilson was laid in his grave. The royal visitor felt his loss as much as any of his personal friends. But the best proof of the sterling worth of this man of God was that the native communities vied with the European in honouring his memory. During his career as an ardent missionary he had come into collision with all the native religions, and the controversies were sometimes, as we have said was the case with the Parsis, personal and bitter. Yet even the Parsis had long before his death forgotten the animosities into which that very zeal, which they certainly admired and imitated, had betrayed their well-wisher, and joined with their native fellow-citizens in mourning the loss of one who had been emphatically the friend of them all, and who, even at the risk of alienating them, had striven for their spiritual welfare according to his own best lights.

Dr. Wilson's loss was keenly felt by those who had come in personal contact with him. Malabari, we have seen, came to know him only during the last few years of his life. But during this period he had seen enough of him to love, trust, and honour him entirely. Dr. Wilson's influence on him must have been very great indeed. To a large extent the two were kindred spirits, though at the opposite poles of life. The old man had run his career of private and public virtues, based on heroic self-sacrifice, and died a martyr to his cause. The young man, too, was of the stuff of which martyrs are made ; but it was probably his intercourse with Wilson that helped him first to discover this for himself. He saw before him a living example of pure and saintly life, such as most of us know of only in the pages of biography. This helped to determine his character and the channel into which his life should run. To him was vouchsafed the grace to rise above mere worldly considerations and to choose the better part. It is not the privilege of many young men to know in the flesh great moving forces like Dr. Wilson. This was Malabari's good fortune, and he made the most of it while it lasted. His own life presents a close resemblance, in many respects, to the life that may be considered his exemplar. Both show the literary instinct very strong in them, and both have shone as authors. In both of them the moral sense predominates over everything else; and prompts them to feats of self-sacrifice. Their life has a fixed purpose, the load-star of their course, and that is to do good to their fellows. If Wilson was what is called a missionary, Malabari is no less a missionary, though without that name. He has a most definite mission, and pursues it vigorously and without flinching. Even in his methods, he is an enthusiastic missionary. He employs all the means available in the present advanced age to further his object, and combines them with other methods prevalent in a former age. Like the enthusiastic preachers of the Middle Ages in Europe, and of many a later day in India and the East generally, he moves about from place to place, leading his campaign, stirring up his followers, organizing committees, winning over opponents by personal example in forbearance and self-sacrifice, and remonstrating with over-zealous friends who would hurry on at too eager a pace and thus endanger the cause. His peripatetic exertions on behalf of social reform may well be compared to the more famous and disastrously active efforts of that fiery hermit who flitted from court to court and nation to nation, with his stirring story of the woes of his fellow-Christians in the home and land of the Bible, and never rested from fanning the animosities he had created into a fierce flame which drew the whole of Europe into its vortex and burned for several centuries. This old peripatetic method Malabari has improved upon by the facilities afforded by railways and other means of locomotion. He added to it, moreover, a method that was unknown in former ages. (The newspaper press is a growth of recent years in India, and this our ' pilgrim reformer' has utilized with unique success to aid his unique campaign. His own journal, pamphlets, leaflets, books, with every other form of publicity, have also been laid under contribution by himself and his followers. Everything, in short, that could help in the cause has been utilized. All this argues zeal such as comes only to those who have a definite mission in life and are entirely possessed by it. The principle of self-effacement, on which Malabari's efforts are based, is something which even Christian missionaries may envy.

As we have said, he possessed the qualities which have helped him to do all this, and become what he is. Wilson's example had great influence upon him for the exercise of these qualities for philanthropic purposes. It is scarcely profitable to speculate on possibilities, but this much could be asserted, that without the direct, though brief, contact he had with that noble character, Malabari would not have been what he has become.

In one respect only Wilson's influence failed of its purpose, at least directly, and in the way he wanted it to act. That was in respect of the young Parsi's conversion to Christianity. Wilson was, above everything, an apostle of the Gospel, and subordinated all purposes to the main one of spreading it wherever and whenever he could. It may, then, be asked, what was the effect on Malabari of his efforts at conversion? So far as outward appearances of Christianity go, he has not been converted. He has not been baptized. He could not be prevailed upon, in spite of every earnest effort, to accept the central dogmas of that faith. The theological, dogmatic part of Christianity he could not honestly accept. And it must have called forth all his strength of mind to resist the effort, so earnest and so persistent, of one who, he was convinced, was working solely for his highest welfare. Malabari's main difficulty was the doctrine of mediation. He believed in salvation by faith and by work, but did not think the mediation of another absolutely necessary. In a note in the *Indian Muse* we learn his views on the subject at this critical time, just after Dr. Wilson's death. 'It hardly seems to be in the nature of things,' says he, 'that Christianity can gain on the subtle Indian intellect. As a race, we have little impulse or emotion in a matter like this; and thus what is readily accepted by the exquisitely-nerved European, as the direct instance of revelation, with us sinks into a burst of pure fanaticism.) *Faith*, which precedes and supersedes *thought* with the devout Christian, and which has been, from time to time, working magically on the most sublime intellects of the West, seldom actuates the heart of the proud Asiatic, who strives to purchase salvation with *work*, and never stoops to accept it as alms, as it assuredly would be if *faith* were to be his only merit. Still it must be borne in mind, that all human work falls short in this as in every other case.' This shows that at a very early age Malabari had pondered over the deep metaphysical problems, not of Christianity alone, but of other religions likewise.

But though he could not accept the dogmas of Christianity, he had imbibed all its true spirit, especially as this was in full harmony with his own nature. If true Christianity is to be found in the life led on this earth by its Founder, and recorded by His loving disciples, and if its dogmas are embodied in His great Sermon on the Mount, then Malabari is a Christian; indeed, all truly good men are Christians. The spirit of charity, which prompted Him to advise His followers to turn the left cheek to be kissed by him who smites the right, and which He himself showed by blessing His persecutors and murderers; the spirit of self-sacrifice and self-denial, of which His whole life and every part of it was the most illustrious example; these Malabari imbibed naturally and without the least hesitation, often with the greatest alacrity. If Christianity imbues people with this its true spirit, and makes them better men, charitable and self-forgetful, it must be said to have achieved its highest practical aim.

This could hardly be done by wrangling over disputed points in metaphysics and theology, by dialectical ability shown in scoring a victory over our opponents, or by mere theoretic preaching of charity and the other virtues, and denouncing not only all the other religions, but all other denominations than one's own. If that noble faith were to triumph by such methods, the triumph would more than defeat its own purpose. Christianity must triumph, not by taking its stand on metaphysics and miracles, for Indian religions have more subtle of the former and much more startling and staggering of the latter, but by the example of practical benevolence which it should inspire, by the pure self-sacrificing lives of its votaries and missionaries. A single true Christian life, lived in the midst of the Indian peoples, would have greater influence, would incline them much more favourably towards the faith, than any amount of preaching or controversy. It may be added that even the small way which Christianity has made in India has been chiefly owing to the saintly lives led by some of its missionaries, their institutions and their everyday work on behalf of the people. The silent example of the life of Ward or Carey, Martyn or Duff, George Bowen or John Wilson, is more eloquent than the best pulpit eloquence, and has had greater influence than the most convincing logic. On the other hand, nothing tends to lower that noble faith in the eyes of the Indians so much as the wranglings and bickerings among the various sects and churches, the lives of ease and worldliness led by some of the ministers, who make of their noble calling a mere profession and do little to exalt it above the other professions.

Christianity has a bright future in India, though the difficulties in its way are enormous. But a faith that started from such humble beginnings, in an obscure corner of Asia, underwent the most terrible persecutions at the hands of one of the mightiest empires in the world, and succeeded at last in conquering its oppressors, in exterminating ancient faiths, and in overspreading the whole of Europe; a faith that has overcome such difficulties and flourished for nineteen centuries, triumphing over the extremes of ignorance and science alike, need not find the obstacles in its path in India insuperable. What we require are the right methods and the right men. There is no reason to doubt that men who stormed the stronghold of ancient Paganism, like the early apostles and their successors, and the martyrs of the primitive Church, will succeed in evangelizing the East.

However, even carried on as at present, the efforts of the missionaries are not fruitless. If they fail to win over the educated classes to the new faith, they certainly succeed in shaking the foundations of the old faiths of the country. The work of destruction is being done effectually; belief in the old religions is giving way among the men who receive a European training. This may not be, perhaps, quite desirable, as it is better to be, in the phrase of Wordsworth, 'a Pagan suckled in a creed outworn,' than to have no creed at all. The old creeds are found to be outworn by them, but they have taken definitely to no new creed. The ground for such a one, however, is being cleared. What that creed is to be, is a matter for speculation. That it will be Christianity in any dogmatic form, one cannot hope. The present agnostic tendency of Européan thought seems to have a fascination for the Indian intellect, and there are signs here and there to show that atheism is spreading and taking the place of the old superstitions. The writings of agnostics and atheists are growing in favour with our academic youths, who seem to consider all religion as superstition, and every creed to be an anachronism.

This is the attitude, we fear, of a majority of 'young India.' But some of the best among them are endeavouring to profit by their acquaintance with the learning and the faith of the West in quite a different way. Knowing the real value of Christianity, and regretting their inability to accept it in its entirety, some of them have tried to engraft it on their own religions, and bring about a fusion of the two. The Brahmo Samaj of Keshub Chunder Sen is an instance of this, and it is a pity that experiment has not met with the support it deserves from the rising generation. Others try to purge their ancient faiths of all superstitious elements, which have settled upon them like a hard crust in the course of ages, and to hold fast to the simple original elements of truth and virtue which they contain. The influence of Western education and faith on Malabari seems to have been of this latter kind. Born and bred a Zoroastrian, he has become, owing to his having come so very close to Christianity, a better and purer Zoroastrian. The new faith enabled him to see many of its noble qualities reflected in his own ancient religion. Christianity must have the credit of this, and Malabari allows it in a liberal measure.

Zoroastrianism, the religion of the Parsis, is one of the most ancient and venerable faiths of the world, and has played a very useful part in the history of Oriental civilization. Founded in a remote age, the antiquity of which is variously placed between the sixth and sixteenth centuries before Christ, by a sage whose insight and foresight were the wonder of the ancient world, that faith influenced an important branch of the great Aryan race, and became the State religion of four great Oriental monarchies. On one occasion it stepped beyond Asia, under Xerxes, and had the battle of Marathon been otherwise decided, it would have overspread the continent of Europe. In its primitive form it was a very simple and pure creed, based on the celebrated formula of good thoughts, good words, and good deeds on the moral side, and on the metaphysical, on the eternal strife waging throughout the Universe between good and evil. But this pure essence has been defiled in its march through the ages by popular ignorance and priest-craft. The sacred writings of Zoroaster were mostly lost, and their place was taken by the inferior writings of later priests, who reduced the primitive faith more or less to a sacerdotal system, with dogmas and rites designed to give importance to their own class. These

later books have come to be called sacred, and are
followed by the ignorant masses. Whilst the very few
original texts that survive, that is, the Gáthás, point
to a sublime nature-worship, and inculcate morality
without any complex theological system whatever, the
later Avesta books, and still later Pahlavi writings and
commentaries, have introduced precepts and notions
foreign to the essence of the religion, and have thus
helped it to degenerate.

Malabari very early saw this degeneration, and his
education and Christian influences sent him back to
the primitive Zoroastrianism of which he saw around
him only a travesty. That primitive faith, he found,
could satisfy the aspirations of his soul as far as these
could ever be satisfied in this life, and he has cherished
it as his most precious possession. This, as we have
said, he owes to Christianity, and is grateful for it.
In characteristic terms he acknowledges his debt to
the religion of Christ: 'At a time when doubt and
distrust are taking the place of reason and inquiry
among the younger generation of India, I feel bound
to acknowledge in my own person the benefits I have
derived from a contact with the spirit of Christianity.
But for that holy contact I could scarcely have grown
into the staunch and sincere Zoroastrian that I am,
with a keen appreciation of all that appeals readily to
the intelligence, and a reverent curiosity for what
appeals to the heart, that much of what is mysterious
to man is not beneath, but beyond, the comprehension
of a finite being.' This has been his attitude towards
Christianity throughout his career, and his remarks in

his latest work on English life and character in its own home, are inspired by the same lively sense of gratitude and admiration, and the same openness to conviction.

Dr. Wilson, then, failed to make him a Christian, but he succeeded in making him a better man, inspired by all that is good and true in the Christian faith superadded to that in his own. And if the venerable missionary had lived longer, he would certainly have been proud of the moral and religious development of his protégé. Malabari is himself surprised how he resisted Wilson's attempts at conversion. His bosom friend, Dr. Bhabha, yielded, became a staunch Christian, and persevered in his new faith in spite of bitter persecution by relatives and friends, and has given himself up to Christian work. Malabari says, in one place, ' If anything could have made me a Christian, it was this friend's example.' Perhaps it was better, his countrymen might reply, that he could not profess Christianity. In that case he would naturally have failed to command the influence he now wields whilst remaining in his community as one of them.

It may be added here that Malabari himself partly agrees with and partly differs from our views as to the effect of Dr. Wilson's proselytizing zeal. Talking to the present writer in the course of a quiet evening stroll, he once observed that Dr. Wilson appeared to him to have opened his campaign too early. The Parsis, as a community, were not prepared to receive his message. This preparedness, what is called *Tauskár*

by philosophers, is essential. The soil of the soul must
be prepared for the reception of the seed of spiritual
life, he continued. But a soldier of God, like Wilson,
burning with zeal, could not wait. Natures like his
cannot brook delay, cannot sit down to calculate. As
regards religion, Malabari went on to say, it is more
or less a matter of heredity, temperament, surrounding,
and of experience. It works differently in different ages,
and on different men. Even on the same man it works
differently at different stages of his life. ' I know not,'
he wound up, with that far-off gaze of his pathetic
eyes, in which faith seems to be constantly struggling
for mastery over doubt, 'if India will become Christian, and when. But this much I know, that the life
and work of Christ must tell in the end. After all,
He is no stranger to us Easterns. How much of our
own He brings back to us, refined and modernized!
His European followers seek Him most for His divine
attributes. To me Jesus is most divine in His human
element. He is so human, so like ourselves, that it
will not be difficult to understand Him, though it is
doubtful if the dogmas preached in His name will
acquire a firm hold on the East.'

Malabari deplored the loss of his friend in a volume
unique in the annals of vernacular literature. He wrote
a series of elegiac lyrics in the same Gujarati as his
first volume, in which he gave vent to his grief. He
recounted, in beautiful verse, the main events in the
life of the great philanthropist, and held up for the
first time before his countrymen the portrait of a
devout Christian who had given up his country and

sacrificed brilliant worldly prospects for the good of the people in a distant land, inspired by no other motive but that of serving God. The influence of such a book cannot fail to be wide and lasting. *Wilson Virah*, as it was named, was recognized by critics as a remarkable work, likely to take a permanent place in literature. It is a collection of lyrics, skilfully pieced together something like the *In Memoriam* of Tennyson, but neither so sustained in interest nor so philosophical. It comes nearer to the two greatest purely elegiac poems in English literature, the *Lycidas* of Milton and the *Thyrsis* of Matthew Arnold, though it is not pastoral in form like these. But the love and admiration for their friends, and the keen sense of loss which breathe through them, are present in the same intense degree, and find vent, in equally poetic terms, in the Indian poem. As a literary effort, *Wilson Virah* marks a distinct improvement on the *Niti-Vinod*, with fewer indications of immaturity and straining after effect. This poem was published three years after the death of its hero, in 1878, and the author's position was by that time fairly well assured.

CHAPTER V.

Journalism in India—*The Indian Spectator*—New Political Activity, unrest and dissatisfaction—Criticism of Government.

BEFORE this elegy was published, and a little after Dr. Wilson's death, an important event occurred, which finally determined Malabari's worldly career. He entered the ranks of journalism, which he has never since left, though often longing to do so. With English education and ideas, it was natural that this most characteristic of English institutions should be introduced into India among the natives. The first newspaper in the country was started more than a century ago in Calcutta, by an Englishman, and for a long time the press was in the hands of English writers alone, who were unconnected with the official class, and who distinguished themselves by freely criticizing the policy of the Government. The latter, however, rightly thought that the country was not yet ripe for a free and unlicensed press, which would be a source of serious anxiety and trouble to the rulers. Some journalists, like the famous Silk Buckingham, who had come from England with notions of liberty unsuited to the country, and who persisted in subjecting the British administration in India to unsparing criticisms

G 2

of all its acts, had to be severely dealt with, and to be sent back to the country better fitted for the reception of liberal ideas. Experienced Anglo-Indian officials, like Elphinstone and Malcolm, who had spent their lives in India, were strongly opposed to allowing the press to criticize the Government at all.

After a time, however, when the British Government seemed to be firmly established and well able to bear, without serious damage, the light of searching hostile criticism, the press was made free at the instance of that enthusiastic lover of liberty, Lord Macaulay, to whom India, and especially the English-educated Indians, owe lasting gratitude. Even before the liberty of the press was granted, by which a great stimulus was given to public journalism in this country, vernacular papers were started by educated natives, who conducted them, of course, in a tentative, timid manner. The first vernacular paper came into existence, nearly eighty years ago, in Bombay, which has thus had the honour of showing the way to the rest of India. It was edited and printed by a Parsi, and this race has ever since been prominently connected with Indian journalism. (With the progress of education among the natives, newspapers began to multiply. The greatest impetus to the press has, however, been given to it only of late, by the manifestation of political activity among the English-educated Indians, which is the most notable feature of public life to-day.

The vernacular press has been the growth of English education in India, and is the main channel of its political activity, the outcome of this education. This newly-educated class give vent to their political aspirations through their journals, which are now to be found in every city and town of the various provinces. The newspaper press has a strong fascination for young men in every country. The youth of India found in it the charm of novelty, as no such thing formerly existed among them. It was almost inevitable, then, that a young man of the ability and literary talents of Malabari should turn to journalism for a profession, and an opportunity soon offered itself. Some enterprising friends, hardly having finished their school career, had the pluck to start a weekly paper, partly political and partly literary and social. They had very simple notions about financing the venture. Confident of their ability to supply good reading, they felt equally sanguine about having plenty of subscribers. One of them seems to have been a sort of business man, as he was a clerk in the service of the municipality. He undertook to find a fair supply of advertisements. Thus, with a very small capital, and with very large expectations, they began to publish, every Sunday morning, a paper somewhat the size of the London *Spectator*, and named after it. This was the beginning of the now famous *Indian Spectator*, which, from such a humble origin, rose to occupy a prominent place in Indian journalism and to become a force in public affairs.

The new paper, like its analogue of London, did not record the events of the week so much as comment on them. And like it, too, it made a distinct feature of essays on social and literary subjects. Malabari was, some time after the start, invited to contribute by the enthusiasts, one of whom, Mr. Ferozesha Pestonji Taleyárkhan, was his intimate school friend, and of whose literary talents he still cherishes a high opinion. This friend, who was the editor in charge, contributed the political notes and articles. Malabari took up the lighter section, and sent in essays on social topics, conceived in his peculiar vein.

The paper was conducted on thoroughly independent lines, free from all party obligations. Its criticisms of all parties alike were trenchant, as coming from young men with great daring and little experience. With characteristic boldness it attacked some of the older heads of the native community, who had rendered good service in the past, but who had, in course of time, grown dogmatic and were losing touch with the new generation. Some of these veteran leaders were known for their unflinching opposition to Government, and constant and uncompromising criticism of all its acts. The *Indian Spectator* would have little to do with such public critics and their line of conduct. But these were gentlemen of established position and influence, who could not be either easily or safely opposed. The young men lacked prudence, though they possessed enough, perhaps more than enough, of courage and dash. Their little weekly was sought to be discredited by its influential opponents, and a dead set was made against it in some quarters. The subscription list, never long, dwindled away. The advertisements, so sanguinely expected, and which, even more than subscriptions, are the outcome of influence and connexions, the very thing our young enthusiasts not only lacked but had arrayed against them, never came. Prospects became gloomier still after a few months. A more serious mishap threatened, and finally wrecked, the spirited venture. The partner, who had put in his small capital in the concern, was by this time disenchanted. He grew importunate in his demands. But the money could not be found. The partners quarrelled and separated. The whole concern was sold off for a nominal sum to a Borah, and the *Indian Spectator* was thus found breathing its last, after a more or less stormy existence.

But though doomed to death, it was fated not to die. The Borah bethought himself that with other things he had also bought the name and goodwill of the paper that had, to all intents and purposes, ended so disastrously; and, with the shrewd business instincts of his race, he wanted to turn this to account. From some source he had heard of the juvenile contributor with literary tendencies, whom he now sought out and made an offer of the goodwill for the trifling sum of Rs. 25. Malabari had no thought whatever of owning a paper, much less of conducting it. But when an old friend like the *Spectator* came seeking him in such a stress, he could not help yielding. Possibly, too, his mind conjured up vistas of public usefulness and importance as editor. Anyhow, he bought the *Spectator* in a singularly auspicious moment. He had known, however, of its struggles under his friends who had zeal and ability, but very little of funds, and endeavoured, if possible, to avoid a repetition of such hardships to himself. He thought himself lucky, therefore, in having secured a capitalist partner, who was ready to advance the money requisite for publishing the new paper, and who is believed to have sent the Borah to the guileless Parsi publicist. This acute Hindu gentleman seized the opportunity of utilizing the paper and the editor's talents, partly for his own purposes and partly in the interests of the public. He advanced the printing charges for a month, promising further a regular supply, in the hope that the paper would become practically his own organ. But he had mistaken his man. The moment our green young journalist saw that he was expected to write at the instance of his capitalist partner, he resolved he would have nothing to do with him. He paid off the debt incurred, with the help of his devoted wife, and became independent again.

Before he thus took up the new paper, Malabari had already served his apprenticeship as journalist under a veteran of the craft, Mr. Martin Wood. We have seen that he had been introduced to this gentleman by Sir Cowasji Jehangier, and was soon utilized by him. Mr. Wood, who had been for a long time editor of the *Times of India*, was then starting a paper of his own, named the *Bombay Review*, in which he wanted to advocate specially the cause of the Native States and the native population of Bombay. He made the young Parsi his coadjutor, who continued for nearly two years to write for the *Review*. But the new weekly, in spite of its editor's ability and influence, could not get on financially. It had to be discontinued

after a brief but eminently useful career. This con-
nexion, however brief, was beneficial to Malabari, as it
gave him the first training under an experienced hand.
It, moreover, enabled him to knock off many of those
charming sketches of life and character in Gujarat,
which were later collected and published in London.
This volume, *Gujarat and the Gujaratis*, was the first
to raise Malabari to the ranks of English authorship.

The *Bombay Review* came to a premature end
soon after the *Spectator* was revived by Malabari.
Mr. Martin Wood spoke of the new editor in very
favourable terms, which show that he had already
discerned the rare qualities which have made both the
journal and its conductor so deservedly famous. The
retiring veteran wrote: ' The editor is peculiarly
fitted for being a trustworthy interpreter between
rulers and ruled, between the indigenous and immi-
grant branches of the great Aryan race. It is easy to
see that he thoroughly understands the mental and
moral characteristics of these two great divisions of the
Indian community, not only as presented in Bombay,
but in other provinces in India. We have always felt
confidence in the sincerity and independence of its
editor. His knowledge of the various castes and
classes of society in Western India is full and exact,
while in aptitude for discussion of social questions he
displays a discrimination and aptness in picturesque
description, and a genuine humour, sufficiently rare.'

After this separation from his respected guide and
friend, Malabari had to undergo a severe trial. Of
money he had little, and a wife and children had to be

supported. His earnings were fair enough for his purposes, but he was careless in money matters, and much of his income was lost to the family owing to his easy good-nature and want of business capacity. Unworthy friends took advantage of this weakness in his character. He helped these men recklessly; and even stood security for some of their debts, which he had ultimately to make good. Thus he became twice involved in pecuniary difficulties, which were intensified by the struggles of the *Indian Spectator*. The strain of the new venture was severe indeed:—' I struggled on,' says he, 'writing, editing, correcting proofs, at times folding and posting copies, and even distributing them in town, going the round in a cab, with the driver delivering the copies as instructed by me.' Such were the struggles through which he has worked his way up to success.

Through all his bitter experiences Malabari has come to believe in the wise saying of Burke, that difficulty is good for man. He is truly himself in the face of difficulties whose magnitude draws out his very best qualities. He is not born to be daunted by obstacles—a fact which he has proved abundantly, and more than once, during his career. In his early struggles with poverty, in this commencement of his journalistic career, and later in his campaign against infant marriages and enforced widowhood—which may well be considered the crowning piece of his life-work— he has shown that he possesses unflinching courage, resolution, and perseverance. This trait of character it may surprise many to find combined with the poetic temperament and a nature so intensely sensitive as his. It is rare, indeed, to find a genuine poet like Malabari engage in active public work, so varied and exacting in its nature. But his poetry seems to have inspired him to do practical good to his fellows by every means in his power; Duty and Action are its key-notes. In his latest volume of Gujarati verse he has a beautiful poem on Duty, which reveals his own springs of inspiration and embodies his gospel of work. ' Duty is devotion : duty is salvation : duty is our final rest in heaven.' This is the burden of his song, which, for moral earnestness and lofty sentiment, comes well up to Wordsworth's famous ode.

He rose superior to all obstacles, and by dint of patient hard work, and with such help as he could obtain, succeeded in firmly establishing his paper. The time when he started on his career as a journalist was favourable for success to rising talent in India. It was the commencement of the viceroyalty of Lord Ripon, who was sent by Mr. Gladstone, on his coming to power in 1880, to reverse the imperialist policy which Lord Lytton had launched upon, and which had proved so disastrous both to the prestige and finances of India. This aggressive policy on the north-west frontier, which partly gave rise to a repressive policy within the country, could not be approved by Indian journalists, who denounced it in terms not always well measured nor sober. The Conservative Government, not relishing the persistent criticism to which its policy was subjected, and being alarmed at the tone of the native press, which it found ' seditious,' curtailed the liberty of the press by a legislative measure passed in hot haste, and thus aimed a blow at public criticism. The political discontent caused by the military and financial disasters in Afghanistan, and the coercion of the native press, were further aggravated by the physical calamity of a famine which raged over the country and carried off several millions of the population. Thus it was with feelings of intense relief that the end of the Beaconsfield Ministry was hailed by the Indians. Mr. Gladstone had shown his distrust of his brilliant predecessor's way of managing the affairs of the Empire in Europe and Asia, and had sent out to India a man totally different from Lord Lytton in opinion and temperament.

Lord Ripon, the new Viceroy, set about the task of repairing the mischief done by his predecessor in foreign as well as domestic affairs. The policy of aggression and interference on the north-west frontier was abandoned. Afghanistan was evacuated. Collision with Russia was shunned, and a conciliatory attitude was assumed towards that country. The finances of India, left in a deranged condition, with a heavy deficit, and burdened by thirty millions of additional debt by the late administration, were rapidly put on a sound basis again, under the guidance of an able and skilful minister, Sir Evelyn Baring, now Lord Cromer, who has since done similar service to the finances of Egypt.

But the most marked departure from the former policy was the attitude of the new Government, and especially its head, towards the natives. Instead of repression and coercion, the latter met with encouragement and help. Public criticism was invited; public opinion welcomed. Public leaders were recognized and consulted. The native press was given back its recently lost liberty; and its opinions, however crude, were carefully considered. The educated natives in every province, struck with the sympathetic tendency of the new Government, began to take a considerably enhanced interest in public affairs. They received an unprecedented impetus in politics, and were almost entirely engrossed by them. Political activity, never before heard of in the country as a whole, manifested itself everywhere in an unmistakable manner. New associations were formed, old ones revived, and the art of agitation introduced with almost all its Western machinery. Monster meetings and monster petitions became common. The platform became an institution. The pamphlet and the placard were put to novel uses.

High hopes and aspirations were thus raised among the small band of educated Indians, who forthwith prepared to put into practice the liberal notions they had imbibed in their schools and colleges under English professors. Whether these hopes will ever be fully realized, whether the educated minority could safely be given all that they want from their rulers; whether they represent really the whole of the various nations of the Indian continent; and whether these have yet arrived at the point where they could be given a measure of active self-government which is demanded for them and in their names—these questions need hardly be discussed here. But that such hopes have been created; that the educated classes are

becoming dissatisfied with the present state of things;
that there is a strong and a strange ferment working
in certain ranks of Indian society, making for unrest
and change; that instead of looking upon the English
rulers as their real benefactors, they are beginning to
view their actions suspiciously, seizing every opportunity of criticizing and censuring, and, in some cases,
of lowering the prestige of their rulers; that the race-
feeling between the rulers and the ruled, instead of
diminishing, has increased with the increase, and
spread, so to say, with the spread of literary education
among our young men; that all this is more or less true
at present, cannot be denied by an impartial political
observer. On the contrary, it must be mournfully admitted by every person who has the good of the Empire
at heart, that the signs are getting worse, that needless
acerbity is shown on both sides, and that influential
mediators are sadly wanting to heal wounds which
are not allowed to close. *Si monumentum quaeris,
circumspice.* Everywhere and all around proofs of this
abound. In schools and colleges and universities, in
debating clubs and associations; in literature, spoken
and written; in newspapers and pamphlets, plays and
novels; in public life, in municipalities and legislative
councils; in private life, in after dinner talk and
friendly converse; in short, in all departments of life,
this new tendency, this mental unrest and dissatisfaction
with the present order, is the one thing conspicuous,
almost aggressive. Why this should be so, why the
class which owes its very existence to the British rule,
and from which additional stability was expected to be

given to it, should seem to be uncompromisingly
opposed to it, should seem to try to belittle the good
done by it; why the official class of Englishmen should
be treated, not as friends of the country and the people,
whom they serve amid great difficulties and at great
sacrifice; why the official class appear to be less in
touch with the people than before, and less able to
distinguish between opponents and enemies, between
critics of their own acts and detractors of the Government, is an inquiry of the most vital importance for
one competent enough to enter upon it.

The Indian press received its greatest stimulus from
this rush of political activity. In fact, from the viceroyalty of Lord Ripon may be dated its second birth.
As we have seen, it existed long before this period;
but its voice was feeble, and its influence but small
owing to its limited constituency. In the new state
of things the press was the first instrument to be
handled by the political party. New papers were
started, both in the vernaculars and in the English
language; old papers that were drooping had new
spirit infused into them. The spirit of organization
was abroad, for the first time, and pervaded the native
press. Its voice became stronger, because united, and
spoke out in no faltering tone. Its circulation increased rapidly, and its influence spread over a much
wider circle than before. Enjoying the fullest amount
of liberty, the papers wrote with a straightforwardness
which was surprising, and at times alarming, when
compared with their former mode. Viewing every
question that arose for discussion from their own point

of view, they criticized the action of the Government freely and boldly. Still more they criticized the action of the officials of the Government, over whom they kept a strict watch. This liberty, newly acquired, and the possession of power and influence, suddenly felt, have led to their abuse in many cases. Interested opposition to Government, and captious and unfair criticism of the whole official class, have become the distinguishing marks of a certain section of the native press, which is mainly responsible for the breach between the races now widening.

Such, then, was the time when the *Indian Spectator* entered upon a new lease of life. It could not but be favourable to both the journal and the journalist. Men of talent saw a career opening for them in politics, either in the press or on the platform. And many of the leading native politicians of to-day came to the front in the early eighties, borne on the new wave of political activity. Malabari participated in this activity and this enthusiasm; but he guided himself by principles of his own, occupying a unique position among his fellow-workers in the same field. From the very first he took a higher view of his profession than most native journalists. He determined not to be an advocate of any one party or cause in politics, but to be a judge. He conducted his paper in an eminently judicial spirit, bearing in mind what is due to all sides of a question. He was firmly impressed with the fact that Truth is many-sided, and he tried to see as many sides of it as possible. In short, he has throughout been a firm supporter of the just and lawful claims of the people, and the educated classes, wielding his pen mainly towards the redress of their grievances. With the people especially he has shown the warmest sympathy, ever using his opportunities to better their condition. Their actual condition at present under the British rule, whether they have really benefited by it, and how the benefit can best be made to reach the lowest classes—these questions have been his special study, for which his intimate knowledge of the country, and his natural inclination for espousing the cause of the weak, have well fitted him. This line of inquiry has taken him to the very root of the problem of the British rule in India and how it affects the people. He has studied the dark side of the rule as well as the bright, and judiciously endeavoured to throw light on the former, as well as to hold up the latter to the appreciation of his less discerning countrymen. This is not difficult for one to whom 'journalism is not a trade, not a business, not even a mere profession, but an avocation, a call, a holy mission.' It is in this spirit that Malabari has worked his *Spectator*, and it is for this reason, mainly, that he has come to be recognized as the prince of Indian publicists. We shall quote one authority here to bear us out—an Englishman whom the advanced politicians of India are proud to reckon as their leader. This gentleman, writing to a friend about the *Indian Spectator* and its editor, observes :—' Lord Ripon did not hesitate to number him amongst his friends, and considered his paper the best and wisest of all the papers edited by natives. Moderation and good sense have been the leading characteristics of the *Spectator*, which, though it has ever consistently supported native interests, has never laid itself out for popular applause, or played the demagogic game . . . It plays a most important part in the national development.'

As a journalist, he has rendered invaluable service to India by his championship of her cause. He has never stooped to conciliate popular whims and prejudices, as many others have done, to the detriment of public morality and independence. Nor has he had anything to do with that carping criticism of the official class, and rank abuse of Englishmen, which have been the characteristics of the majority of irresponsible writers during the last decade. Malabari's innate sense of justice and charity has always guided him in his journalistic career, and made it the conspicuous success that it has been. During times of wild excitement and heated controversy he has kept his head cool, often trying successfully to calm the public mind and lead it to wise conclusions. Perhaps the most notable instance of this was Malabari's service on a critical occasion, during the agitation which is known as the Ilbert Bill Controversy. The compromise, by which the bitter differences that had arisen between the native and the European communities in India were sought to be made up, was, as first imperfectly announced, on the point of being violently criticized and rejected by the native press and the public on this side, as it had already been condemned in Bengal and elsewhere; and the Government was on the point of being placed in an unenviable position. But Malabari, besought by the authorities to suspend judgement till further information was supplied, exerted his influence with the Press and the representatives of public opinion generally to think better of it.

On such critical occasions the *Indian Spectator* has filled a distinct place in contemporary politics. The foremost public men in India and England have recognized its services, speaking in high terms of its policy and methods. What Lord Cromer wrote, when Finance Minister in India, strikes the keynote of its excellence. ('I always read your paper with interest for two reasons, first, because it represents the interests of the poorer classes; secondly, because it is opposed to class and race antagonism. The last point is especially important in this country.' Yes, this last point is really of exceptional importance in India, where class and race antagonism is becoming more intense, where some of the various races which inhabit our continent hate one another with a hatred that is made explicable only by their antecedents, and which of late years has occasionally shown itself in violent outbursts. The hatred, for instance, between the two great races, the Hindu and the Mahomedan, has affected the impartiality of a portion of the native press, which deals in mutual recriminations and aspersions. Many of the papers being in the hands of the landed and moneyed classes, the interests of the poor ryots are but scantily looked after by them, and on occasions when they collide directly with their own, no scruple is felt in sacrificing them. This was clearly seen at the passing of the Bengal Tenancy Bill, which, though it tried to remove the causes of misunderstanding between the tenant and the landlord, was bitterly opposed by the native papers in the interests of the zamindars or landlords. The same papers, which had only a little while before praised Lord Ripon to the skies, decried him for this his last and perhaps justest piece of legislation. Such inconsistency is not to be wondered at.

Of the *Indian Spectator*, however, it may be honestly said that it has never viewed any public question from the point of view of class or race. If ever it has been compelled to do so, it has taken the side of the poorer class and the weaker race. Justice and moderation have been the cardinal points of its policy and the secret of its success and influence. When occasion required, it has never feared to speak out and condemn injustice, from whatever quarter proceeding. It has been the staunchest supporter of the ruling race. But when the rulers have been found to err, in its opinion, it has always exposed the error and raised its voice in favour of amending it. The British Government, like all Governments, must have its faults—faults of policy and faults of individual officers. And the *Spectator* has always been on the alert to bring these to the notice of the Government, who acknowledge the great utility of such criticism. An official, here and there, who has been exposed for bullying or harassing the people under his charge, may have become a personal enemy of the critic. But, on the whole, the ruling class appreciates the immense importance of the kind of criticism of its policy and acts which papers like the *Spectator*, and men like Malabari, offer to its notice. The British Government is a foreign government in India, and apt, like all such, to be unsympathetic, owing to the unsympathetic nature of the British, but much more to want of touch with the masses and lack of knowledge of their ways and wants. Legislative measures, initiated with the best intentions by the rulers, are likely to be misunderstood, and in the end generally miscarry, to their great surprise. Many a benevolent act of the English has been misconstrued by the ignorant masses, and felt by them as quite the reverse, simply because the rulers cannot enter into the state of feelings and ideas of the ruled. They thus need, in a peculiar manner, the aid of well-trained and well-meaning native critics, to act as mediators and interpreters, who, while they try to convince the ruled of the good intentions of the rulers, also bring to the notice of these latter the prejudices and peculiar notions of the former, which it would be unstatesman-like to ignore. The class of such natural mediators is, unfortunately, very small, and Malabari, with his *Spectator*, may be said to be its best type and repre-sentative. Being an Indian of the Indians, and know-ing the ways and habits of his countrymen intimately, and feeling for their welfare as few others could feel, he employs his advantages chiefly in helping the foreign Government in their task of governing them.

Perhaps the most valuable of Malabari's services to India, as journalist, may be traced to his private correspondence with the higher officials of Government and the authorities in England. Many are the men whose Conservative prejudice he has overcome by gentle remonstrance; whom he has sometimes won over to the fold of Liberalism so far as Indian politics are concerned. The effect of one such conversion could hardly be over-estimated. But it is too early yet to estimate the value of this side of Malabari's political activity.

It was somewhere about this period, or a little earlier, that he came in contact with Mr. D. E. Wacha, whose good offices he never tires of acknowledging, publicly and in private. Mr. Wacha seems to have written largely at the time for the *Indian Spectator*; and, what was more useful, helped to keep its finances going. The *Spectator* was too independent to make two ends meet—a merit or a misfortune that has clung to it all through its career. And Mr. Wacha, with his quick sympathy and knowledge of men and affairs, seems to have determined that such an organ of genuine public opinion should not die. He induced two Parsi friends, Messrs. J. R. Mody and J. N. Tata, to indemnify the proprietor against his losses for a year each. Mr. Mody further accommodated the struggling journalist with a loan to pay off the arrears. 'This marked,' says Malabari, 'a turning-point in my career as a journalist.' Among other friends Malabari speaks enthusiastically of Mr. Hume, Mr. Dadabhai Naoroji, Mr. Ardasir Framji, and Sir W. Wedderburn. 'I could write a volume,' he adds, 'about each of my friends—about his friendly, brotherly, fatherly interest in one who differs from him as strongly on some questions as on others he agrees with him. Sir W. Wedderburn is the only Englishman from whom I have accepted money aid for the *Spectator* (many others have offered to help me in this and other directions). I was never so touched as when Sir William pressed his offer, arguing, when all other arguments had failed, that unless I accepted his brotherly offer, he would not believe I treated him really as a brother. And a brother, indeed, he has been.' With good times coming he paid off the liabilities incurred by the paper; and in the case of friends who refused to be repaid, he spent the money on deserving public objects, in the names of the original donors!

CHAPTER VI.

Book on Gujarat, a true Picture of life in Town and Village—Translations of Max Müller's Hibbert Lectures dealing with the Religions of India.

THE immense and intimate knowledge of the land and its people, thus acquired, he obtains and keeps up by prolonged tours. His is not the ordinary journalist's information, picked up at third hand from books. He has always delighted to be in living touch with the people, to observe all aspects of their life, from the highest to the lowest, from the Rajah's court to the ryot's hut, to see with his own eyes their condition under the present rule, and to hear with his own ears their views about the rulers, and their grievances, real and imaginary, against the Government. Born among the people, and mixing with them from his earliest years, he has always been careful to keep himself in the closest touch with them. The objection, usually brought against the newly created class of natives, that they do not know the real condition of their poorer countrymen, from whom they are alienated by their European training, cannot be urged against Malabari. Few men know the real people of India, and especially the people of his own province of Gujarat, so intimately. Fewer still have favoured either their own countrymen or the rulers with the results of their knowledge. Malabari gave the result of his first tours in a series of sketches of men and manners contributed to the *Bombay Review* and the *Indian Spectator.* They were much appreciated at the time of publication, and helped to bring their writer into greater notice. Later, at the suggestion of competent critics, they were rescued from the oblivion of a newspaper file, to be published in a volume, entitled *Gujarat and the Guja-ratis,* by Messrs. Allen, of London. This book first revealed the extraordinary command of the writer over English, all the more surprising in one who had received but a poor education and had read but little of its literature. The ease and vigour with which many educated Indians of to-day wield the language of their rulers is really remarkable, and is a matter of wonder to Englishmen themselves, as well as to the other Europeans who despair of attaining perfection in the highly idiomatic and irregular speech of England. This is chiefly owing to the assiduous attention the Indians pay to English; and mastery over the foreign tongue is often obtained at the sacrifice of their mother tongue. But Malabari is not an assiduous student, nor a learned scholar. His reading has been con-fessedly very limited and desultory. With literature in its wider sense he is practically unacquainted. The great masterpieces, to which students give their days and nights, have been skipped by him. His study of Gujarati literature must have taken up not a little of his scanty leisure. He has cultivated that literature to some extent, and, as we have seen, written works in it

which will live as long as that simple dialect lasts.
Under these circumstances his power over the English
language appears phenomenal. It can only be explained
by his genius. The language comes to him naturally,
and his strength of expression and felicity of phrase
are instinctive. It is the privilege of genius to seize
at once, and by a short cut, what ordinary understand-
ings grasp only after laborious efforts, and even then
imperfectly. Malabari has such genius, and it shines
forth not only in his exquisite style, but also in his
thoughts, which are always more or less original. He
also possesses what is the usual concomitant of genius,
what a great teacher of our days, Carlyle, calls the
essence of all real greatness, the unconsciousness of
possessing it. A friend, who is himself a shrewd
observer and a cultured critic, and who has watched
Malabari's career from the beginning, calls him an
unconscious genius, if ever there was one. Some of
the larger problems of metaphysics, which he had himself pondered over long and intently, and at whose
partial solution he had arrived after deep reading and
still deeper thinking, Malabari, he says, innocent of
any philosophical reading, saw at a glance, going to
their very heart, and offering explanations which coin-
cided with the theories of some of the greatest thinkers.
This genius has not had full opportunity to show itself
in literature. For Malabari has always tried to be
a man of action, rather than a man of letters or of
speculation. Still, it can be seen plainly in the little
that he has published. Nearly every book of his
bears the traces of an original and vigorous mind.

The volume on *Gujarat and the Gujaratis* is also stamped with the genius of the author. He has observed and seized all the real and essential traits of Gujarati character. It is the real living men and women that he portrays, in their strength as well as weakness, and not the mere outward husk of dress and manners with which most writers regale us when writing on such a subject. He presents his observations in a style which is genuine and eminently readable. This comes out of truth to nature, both in the matter and the manner; there is little that is artificial or unnatural about the book. He looked upon human nature round about him with his own natural eyes, without the aid of the spectacles of books, and depicted it in simple, natural terms that came to him spontaneously. The book is a reflex of the author in a high degree. Humour of a rich vein pervades it. And in humour the man also abounds. Those who know him but slightly may not credit Malabari with this rare gift. But closer contact reveals the predominant element of the humorous in his character. 'The writer,' says a critic of this book, 'is truly a humorist in the best sense of the word. He proposes, to quote Thackeray, "to awaken and direct your love, your pity, your kindness, your scorn for untruth, pretension, and imposture. Your tenderness for the weak, the poor, the oppressed, the unhappy." To the best of his means and ability, he comments on almost all the ordinary actions and passions of life. He takes upon himself to be the week-day preacher, so to speak. Accordingly, as he finds, and speaks, and feels the truth best, we regard him, esteem him, sometimes love him.'

Gujarat and the Gujaratis is replete with human interest, full of pictures drawn from the life with rare fidelity and tact. In this respect Malabari comes up to another great writer of our day, Mr. Rudyard Kipling, who excels in describing many phases of life and character, as they are actually to be found in this work-a-day world, in the language of the persons themselves, with all its irregularity and uncouthness. Malabari has had a harder task before him. Kipling has described Englishmen in the English language, for the nervous speech of Mulvaney, with its eccentricities and peculiarities, is, after all, English. Malabari had to depict his countrymen in foreign colours, to translate the thoughts and words of simple Indians in the language of their rulers. Much of the innate force and humour must necessarily evaporate in this process. But our author has succeeded in retaining enough of both while conveying them through a foreign medium.

It seems to have been his object to paint the character of the people in almost all phases and relations. He has selected his typical subjects from all ranks and walks of life, and presented each in his own sphere, with his natural environment. *Quidquid agunt homines, votum, timor, ira, voluptas, gaudia, discursus*— all that the Gujaratis do and are, their ideas, superstitions, fashions, foibles, and frivolities—these form the staple of his book. It requires gifts of a very high order to understand human character aright and to depict it as it is. Even persons with whom we come in close contact, whose actions we observe, and whom we can interrogate personally, are as a rule but partially known to us. Each of us must, in many points, be a puzzle to his neighbour. Nay, each is a puzzle to himself. 'Know thyself' was the first command of the ancient philosopher to man, and this knowledge is attained by most of us the latest. Thus, if it be so hard to know ourselves and our neighbours as we really are, how much more difficult must it be to know peoples who are separated from us by the barriers of race, religion, and language ?

The English feel this difficulty in India at every turn. They cannot, with all their patience and sagacity, understand the character of the peoples whom they have to govern. There is a wide gulf yawning between the two. Then the opportunities of fathoming the Indian character are also few. That character is to be seen at its best in the villages which remain now what they were hundreds of years ago, untouched by the civilization of the Western rulers. The Indian, as he is seen in the towns and cities, where alone the Englishman generally sees him, is not the true Indian, but a mixture of Eastern and Western influences. Malabari knows this difficulty of the rulers, and traces to their ignorance many of the errors which shallow and prejudiced Indian critics attribute to their selfishness and want of principle. In his *Gujarat* he offers his own intimate knowledge of the people to the rulers, who can glean from its pages much that they want but can rarely get from their personal experience. Not

only are the home life, and views, and habits of the
people minutely and accurately described, but the
foreigner is warned against being misled by those self-
seeking subordinates and others who hang about the
official camp, and give out just those views and facts
which they know would be pleasing to the masters.
These are very humorously exposed in *Gujarat*, and
it will be the fault of the young Civilian alone if he
allows himself to be imposed upon by such parasites.
The book, indeed, should be invaluable to those new-
comers whose lot has been cast in the province of
Gujarat, and who have to govern its mild but very
peculiar population.   Copies of it should be found in
every Civilian's kit; he would be wise to study it as
he studies his Regulations and Codes.

Gujarat and the Gujaratis was, of course, a success.
It has gone through several editions, and brought the
writer money as well as fame.   Competent Anglo-
Indian statesmen acknowledge its high merits, especially
its usefulness to the rulers.   They urge the writer to
do for the other provinces of India what he has done
for his own Gujarat.   It would be well if such books
were published.   It is no exaggeration to say that the
task of governing the country would be to a large
extent simplified thereby.   As it is, *Gujarat* stands
alone, and Malabari has not followed it up with the
desired volumes.   Perhaps he has shrunk from the
task, because he does not know the other parts of
India so intimately as his mother province.   But still,
his knowledge of the whole country is almost unrivalled,
obtained mostly at first hand during his prolonged

and well-planned tours, or 'campaigns,' as he half-humorously calls them.

Tours have been with him one of the chief means of achieving his objects. He undertakes them, not for pleasure, but as a matter of duty. He rightly thinks that public opinion should be stirred, formulated, and organized by the leaders personally visiting the centres of thought and activity, guiding, encouraging, checking, and controlling. With the spirit of the true missionary in him, he goes about the country regardless of personal comfort, thinking only of his cause. Not of a robust constitution, he has been struck down many a time on his tours, and saved with difficulty, sometimes after prolonged suffering. His first tour was, as we have seen, over Kathiawad, for the journal started by his friend, Mr. Martin Wood. His next two tours were planned on a much larger scale, and were undertaken for a higher purpose.

This purpose was his project of translating into the vernaculars Prof. Max Müller's Hibbert Lectures on the *Origin and Growth of Religion as illustrated by the Religions of India.* It has been Malabari's aim throughout his life to try to bring the East and the West closer, to unite them by the bonds of knowledge and sympathy. He has pursued this aim steadily in his own works. In Prof. Max Müller's works he found the same aim predominating. And he therefore resolved to bring them to the notice of his countrymen in their own languages. 'Prof. Max Müller,' says he, 'has laboured all his life to bring about a union amongst nations. That union has long been aimed at.

A marriage between East and West was arranged
even before the days of the illustrious William Jones.
In that work of union you trace the hand of a higher
Power than that of man. Modern Indian history
teaches you that. But I may say that Max Müller
and his contemporaries have contributed largely to
bringing to the surface the practical results of that
process of, let us hope, progressive union. By his
works he has given new birth, so to say, to Sanskrit;
he has resuscitated, I say, he has helped to regenerate,
the language and literature of our land.' In a spirit
of enlightened sympathy, Prof. Max Müller has pointed
out to Europeans all that is good in the religions of
India. On the other hand, he candidly shows to the
Indians the defects and errors of their creeds, and
warns them against overvaluing them and interpreting
them as they were never meant to be interpreted.
The Hibbert Lectures embody the substance, so to
say, of all that Max Müller had to say on Indian religions, based on his life-long study of these as well as
of the religions and philosophic thought of the West.
Even independently of this, they are an important
contribution to metaphysical speculation, inasmuch as
the author discusses in them the possibility of religion
in the light of modern science, and takes the history
of religion in India merely to illustrate this central
problem. 'I might define,' he writes, 'my object by
saying that it was a reconsideration of a problem, left
unsolved by Kant in his *Critique of Pure Reason*,
after a full analysis of the powers of our knowledge
and the limits of their application. Can we have

any knowledge of the transcendent or supernatural?
. . . My object was to show that we have a perfect
right to make one step beyond Kant, namely, to
show that our senses bring us into actual contact with
the Infinite, and that in that sensation of the Infinite
lies the living germ of all religion [1].'

It was Malabari's plan to publish translations, in the
principal vernaculars, of a series of European works,
which would help to give shape to his idea of the
union of East and West. Prof. Max Müller's work
was chosen to commence the series, both on account
of its intrinsic merit and of the high reputation of
the author among Indians. Malabari visited various
towns and native states to interest influential people
in his project, and to obtain the necessary funds.
Men like Keshub Chunder Sen, Rajendralala Mitra,
and others, favoured the idea. They believed, with
the enthusiastic projector, that these translations
would bring about a gradual religious revival such
as the country sadly requires. ' India wants nothing
so much as a religious revival, or rather a restoration.
There is no real unity for the nation except through
one faith ; political unity is uncertain. The struggle
lies in future between a new religion for the people
and revival of the old. And to a consummation of
the latter, which will be through a natural process,
I believe that the labours of Max Müller will contribute more than of any other living authority.'
Malabari laboured strenuously for his object. He
travelled far and wide ; wrote, spoke, addressed the

[1] *Biographical Essays*, pp. 160-162.

people, interviewed Rajahs and nobles.' But little practical good has resulted from his efforts. He has succeeded in publishing the Gujarati, Marathi, Bengali, and Hindi versions. The Sanskrit was condemned as unreliable, and the Tamil has not yet been published. It argues very little for the real advancement of the Indians when schemes like this, which required but a moderate sum of money and only average literary talents, have to languish for want of adequate support from them, though the highest names were enlisted on its side.

Sir William Hunter was amongst the first, in India, to appreciate the value of these translations; and he did much, as President of the Education Commission, to popularize the scheme. Sir William has, indeed, been Malabari's staunch friend and supporter almost from the beginning of his career. He has cheered our hero in moments of despondency, and used his pen in the public press, and his voice in the Council of the Empire, to further his political no less than his social and literary gospels. 'Once or twice,' says Malabari, 'I would have broken down but for the sympathy of this gifted civilian.'

CHAPTER VII.

Social Reform, Malabari's life-work—The Position of Indian Women—
The Marriage Question—The Age of Consent Act.

EVEN the slight achievement in the field of literary
and religious revival described above is mainly due
to Malabari's perseverance. For what we may call
dogged persistence is the most striking trait in his
character. What he has once resolved upon he will
anyhow carry through. Difficulties, however great,
he minds but little. If man can overcome them, he
will. He is baffled only by superhuman obstacles.
'Opposition,' he once said to the present writer, 'only
serves to rouse me, and makes me strive the harder.'
Tenax propositi may very justly be said of him. It is
this tenacity that has enabled him to overcome almost
superhuman obstacles, and do what good he has done
to his country during his brief lifetime. The work
which he now undertook was one which called forth
all his best powers. It was a work which only his
unwillingness to accept defeat could have carried
through. The question, when he took it up, was not
at all within the range of practical politics, and his
advocacy of it was set down as quixotic. But within
a few years he made it the burning topic of the day,
moved the Government that was at first immovable,

and succeeded in obtaining a practical, though, unfortunately, but a partial solution of it.

This was the question of Social Reform—aptly described by Miss Nightingale as ' perhaps the greatest reform the world has yet seen '—with which Malabari has wholly identified himself, for which he may be said to have lived, and for which he is ready to die, if need be. People in England cannot easily understand this question of Indian social reform, or the extremely arduous nature of the efforts made to bring it about. The social reform of which we have to speak is of a very elementary character. On account of the complex nature of the social organization, and the long duration of the abuses it has given rise to, the task of reform of even the simplest kind becomes very hard and unpopular. India is rigidly conservative in this respect. Nothing is so popular as the doctrine of *laissez faire.* Social abuses, which nowhere else would have been allowed to exist for any length of time, have been tolerated here for ages with characteristic indifference. Customs with a ruinous tendency, once introduced, take root in India, and are surrounded by a halo of authority. If left to themselves, these customs flourish with all the sanctity of religion. In India every custom, however unintelligible or indefensible, is sheltered under the name of religion ; and the attempt to reform it is taken as an attempt against religion, and denounced as impious. The priestly class, which wields an authority in social matters that is unknown even in the most priest-ridden countries of the West, stands up for these abuses and objectionable customs, and brings its enormous influence to bear, directly as well as indirectly, upon those who would try to reform them. The hold which the priests have upon the female members of the family is used against the reformers, who are thus confronted with bitter opposition in their own homes. The complex machinery of caste, which unites Hindus and holds them as in a dead man's embrace, is set against them. The horrors of excommunication hang constantly over their heads. The social reformer's task is thus of a most trying nature. Many a stout heart has been broken under the strain of persecution. A man may not care for himself; he may, in his own person, defy any persecution, however bitter : but when his whole family is condemned along with him, and severed from all intercourse with the society around them—when, for his zeal, his near and dear ones are made to suffer with him—nothing short of heroism can bear him up. It is unreasonable to expect such heroism from many. Karsandas Mulji, a Hindu of Gujarat, showed such courage in the last generation, and for a long time defied caste and superstition. But he, too, had to yield at last. His last days were embittered by the helpless state to which his family had been reduced. He died in grief and solitude. Caste had proved too strong for his individual efforts. His family could not defy it. They retracted, and underwent a humiliating penance in order to be taken back into the fold of their caste. Superstition and bigotry thus triumphed. A terrible lesson was taught to all recusants and reformers in Gujarat. Few dared to follow

in the steps of Karsandas. Yet, what was the offence
for which he and his family suffered? The head and
front of it was a voyage across the seas to England.
A man may cross the Indian Ocean and go 'to Africa,
and still remain an orthodox Hindu. The sanctity
of caste is not affected by this. But let him go to
Europe and his caste as well as creed is lost in the
sea. His caste, that most sacred thing about him,
the one thing needful to be saved, is lost, and he is
unfit to be a Hindu. Nay, if Hinduism had its own
way, he would be unfit even to live. The man, then,
who dared to cross the water and visit England,
became that incurable sinner, the social reformer.
This might sound strange to English ears: yet this
easy and elementary reform, as it must appear to
foreigners, was fraught with grave danger to the rash
one who ventured upon it.

The caste prohibition against going to Europe
seems puerile, and not very harmful in itself. But
the task of social reform, which Malabari undertook,
was by no means harmless. It touched the position
of women in India. This question has been acknowledged to be the most pressing of the Indian social
questions of our day, and is at the root of them all.
The future of society is based mainly on woman, and
according as she occupies an exalted or degraded
position in it, its stability and moral worth are esti-
mated. Malabari's great object is the regeneration
of his country under the peaceful sway of Britain.
Education is spreading wide, chiefly among the men.
But he rightly holds that the status of the women is

the key of the whole situation. Unless the women are educated and emancipated from the bonds of ignoble customs, there can be little hope for the future. The family is the unit of the State, and the family is based on the mother and the wife. Within their sphere, and this is a very important one, women in India are supreme and all-powerful, in spite of their ignorance. In their present state this power which they wield is wrongly applied, sometimes even to thwart the efforts of their own benefactors. If they become enlightened they will employ their influence in the right channels and for a worthy purpose. The influence of women in India is well illustrated by the saying of an educated leader of Hindu society, that it is easier to defy Her Majesty's Secretary of State than to defy one's own mother-in-law. 'In their own households,' remarks Miss Florence Nightingale with true insight, 'be it in hut or palace, even though never seen, they hold the most important moral strongholds of any women on earth. Supported by custom, Indian women are absolute within their sphere.' The influence of women being so strong and far-reaching, it is all the more essential that they should be educated and enlightened, and thus be made to share, so far as may be, in the blessings of British civilization. But the Oriental's ideas on the subject of educating women are peculiarly narrow. Although in practice woman holds a very influential and important position in the household, yet in theory her status is very degraded. She is not the mate and companion of man, but his servant and slave. She must be in a subordinate position, therefore she must be kept in ignorance. To educate her is considered almost a sin. There are current among the people many absurd superstitions about the spread of knowledge among women; what dire calamities to the race, physical and moral, will follow such an impious attempt! Still, in spite of opposition, female education has made some progress in the country, especially in the large cities, during the present generation. A fair percentage of girls have been returned as school-going in the last census, and there are signs that the percentage will be higher at the end of the present decade.

Education is a good agency for raising the status of women. But the women of India are not merely in a state of ignorance. They are also, as we have explained, in a state of servility, a sort of bondage. Emancipation from this servile state must, then, precede their education. The social evils and disabilities under which they suffer must be first removed if they are sought to be enlightened and educated. Prominent among these social evils of Indian society are infant marriages and enforced widowhood. These two, which follow one from the other and are closely connected, have taken deep root and done infinite harm to the race. Marriage is considered by the Hindus the most sacred and essential act in a woman's life. Every other consideration must give way to this. It is the most solemn duty of the parents to have their daughter married. An unmarried daughter is the greatest curse of the family. She is unhappy herself, and the cause of daily misery to her relatives. The Hindu believes that there is no salvation for him without marriage and male issue. The gates of the other world can be entered only through marriage. This institution being thus of such a vast importance, it is easy to imagine the haste with which parents want to dispose of their daughters in marriage. The haste is not limited even to the age when the girl is fairly grown up and becomes fit to undergo the cares of maternity. Owing to the prevalence of certain absurd customs, there is a scarcity of husbands, an evil which is intensified by the restriction of marriage within a very limited circle. Parents, therefore, have often to find husbands for their daughters as soon as these are born. The result is the system of infant marriages, which, as the late Mr. Justice Telang admitted, is all but universal in India.

These marriages in infancy are harmful in themselves in many ways; they prove disastrous to the race, owing to several other customs existing side by side. Marriage is a sacrament, and therefore indissoluble. But the husband may marry another wife, or more than one, in the lifetime of his first wife. This is one cause of unhappiness. Then there is the disparity of age, temperament, education; there is also the risk of disease and death. Altogether, the marriage is about as foolish and precarious an arrangement as it is possible for superstition to devise. As regards age, a child of seven, even less, is sometimes married to a man of fifty or sixty. What a future the poor child-wife has before her! Before she comes to the age of discretion the old husband may die; and she is a wife no longer, but a widow! Infant marriages thus lead to infant widowhood, and widowhood, painful for all women, is much more painful to the Hindu woman, considering the age at which she generally becomes a widow, and the pains and penalties attaching to the state of widowhood.

According to modern Hindu custom and usage a widow is not allowed to marry again. Though a man may marry several wives at one and the same time, a woman is allowed to marry but once, and if she loses her husband she has to pass the rest of her life, however young, in a state of enforced celibacy. A widow is considered as scarcely to belong to society. She is held a sinner, and her presence is shunned as inauspicious. Her misfortune is often taken for a crime. She is made to bear all the outward marks of widowhood, not only as regards dress, but further by being deprived of her beauty. Her hair, the chief ornament of a woman, the essential element in her beauty, is removed by force, and she is made to pass the rest of her days in this unnatural condition. She also suffers under several legal disabilities. She has no real control over her husband's property, very little actual share in it. She depends for bare maintenance on the family, by whom she is looked down upon as a burden and a nuisance.

Thus, infant marriage and enforced widowhood are connected evils. The girl is married in infancy. If the husband dies, she is compelled to remain a widow to the end of her days, and to sacrifice life and all life's happiness at the shrine of superstition. This double curse undermines society, both physically and morally. Infant marriage leads to early maternity. The wife becomes a mother before she has herself hardly ceased to be a child. The growth of mind as well as body is arrested by this forced and unnatural process. The mother having had no time to develop in a natural way, the child also must be a weakling, even if it survives its birth. The race has thus deteriorated in the course of generations. The physical deterioration of a large portion of the Hindu community is chiefly due to this custom of infant marriages. Enforced widowhood, again, is the cause of moral degradation in not a few cases. A glance at the census will suffice to show how enormous is the extent covered by infant marriage and enforced widowhood, especially among what are called the higher classes.

Such being the great evils of Hindu society, it would be surprising if no attempt were made by the newly educated class to remedy them. Several Hindu gentlemen have endeavoured to paint the evils for the community in all their ghastly forms. Others have proved conclusively that the ancient scriptures do not enjoin infant marriages and do not force perpetual widowhood on girls, but permit of remarriage. The most notable among these was Pandit Ishwar Chunder Vidyasagar of Bengal, a liberal-minded scholar and philanthropist. Many stray attempts were made by him and other heroic souls to break the force of ignorance and superstition. But nothing substantial came of them. Hindu society seemed incapable of reform from within. A strong impetus from outside was needed. And this came now from a neighbouring quarter.

Malabari had from his early days felt the deepest sympathy with Hindu society. Though born a Parsi, he had inherited from his mother an almost incredible attachment for Hindus. She had come in close contact with her Hindu friends and neighbours, and treated them as her kith and kin. The boy had seen his mother tending Hindu children, visiting Hindu widows, and making herself generally useful to all, of whatever caste or creed. This had left an indelible impression on his mind and heart, and he followed the noble example, if not with greater intensity, at least over a wider sphere of usefulness. The woes of the Hindu widow were known to him well enough. In his earliest volume of verse he has sung pathetically of them, and sworn, like a knight-errant of old, to eradicate them some day. In his boyhood he had witnessed some heartrending results of premature marriage and compulsory widowhood. These haunted him during day, and startled him from sleep at night. 'The sights burnt themselves into my brains,' he explained to a friend just before undertaking his crusade. 'It is not merely that I *know* the miseries of widowhood,' he protested to another friend, 'not merely that I *feel* them, feel *for* and *with* the widow; I *am* the widow for the time being.' This may well be believed of one with his intense feeling, who throws his whole heart and mind into the cause he has espoused. It is this eagerness to work and suffer for others that, above everything else, makes him out to be a hero. If this is the essence of chivalry, Malabari is indeed the most chivalrous of India's sons. Anyhow, it is true charity that prompts him, charity of a higher order than that which enables the rich or the powerful to give a fraction of their superfluity to others. In the words of a distant and therefore disinterested observer, Malabari 'has given his life and fortune away to the cause of the weak.' In undertaking the cause of the Hindu child-wife and child-widow, he did not for a moment think that it was the cause of an alien race he was to champion. He considered himself bound to the suffering race by closer ties than those of blood or creed. True charity knows of no creed and no blood. Its object is to alleviate human suffering wherever found. Precedence is given by it, not to a kinsman and co-religionist, but, to quote our reformer, 'to him whose need is the sorest.' Natures like his do not pause to inquire whether the sufferer is Hindu, Parsi, Mahomedan, or Christian. It is enough for them to know the misfortune to be able to feel the need of removing it. Besides, his own community had suffered from the same evils, and was partly suffering from them still. But he rightly thought that Hindu society, with whom the evils arose, and among whom they flourished, needed immediate help. The Parsis, being a compact and energetic body, were able to look after their own affairs, and had, with little extraneous aid, removed several social abuses. Malabari saw the lack of this spirit of self-help among his Hindu neigh-bours, as he also saw the causes of it, and resolved to bring them what brotherly help he could.

He therefore stepped back from the line of literary and political ambition, to give himself up to the humbler rôle of social reformer. This involved immense self-sacrifice. There is little that he could not have achieved as politician and man of letters. As it is, his literary talents, hampered though they are by practical work, have shone brightly whenever he has cared to disclose them. In politics, too, he would have risen to a prominent position, though he is meant by nature to be a statesman rather than a politician. He would have obtained honours and emoluments without stint. But for the success of his cause he preferred to pass them by.

He has given up the last ten years of his life to his self-imposed task of duty. After silent sympathy and careful watching, he came before the public in 1894 with his now famous 'Notes' on Infant Marriage and Enforced Widowhood. His object was not to ask for Government interference in these matters, for he knew such a demand would be premature and vexatious. He submitted the notes for consideration to high officials and influential representatives of the people, and desired to ascertain the drift of opinion on the subjects, and on the advisability or otherwise of interference. Persons in the position of the Viceroy and his Councillors, Governors, Lieutenant-Governors, and others warmly approved of his zeal in this cause, acknowledged the two questions to be of first importance, and sympathized with his efforts to remove the evils of society. But they were not in favour of Government interference at that stage. Until the people, or their representatives, first moved in the matter and asked Government to intervene, they could do little. They advised Malabari to sound non-official public opinion more widely, and to induce it to bring the subject before the rulers of its own accord. He took this advice, and forthwith opened his crusade. He undertook extensive tours through the country, to organize opinion on the questions and to arrange for a general appeal to the Government. His labours were incessant. Associations were started and committees formed in the principal centres of thought. Deputations and petitions were got up. In short, a band of kindred spirits were gathered around him, who worked loyally and enthusiastically for this national object. Nearly every province, from the Punjaub to Mysore, was visited, and enlisted on his side. The spirit of the true missionary was stirred in him. Malabari, as a public man, appears at his best during this crusade.

The result of all these exertions was that within a few years the question of social reform, which was formerly dismissed with an expression of conventional sympathy, came up before the Government for practical solution. The Indian Government obtained what it had wanted. Strong memorials and petitions went up to it, asking for some sort of action on its part. But still, the British Indian Government, with its traditional caution and circumspection, hesitated to act. Meanwhile, also, the reactionary elements of Hindu society had made a stir. The orthodox party shielded the objectionable custom of infant marriage under the name of religion, and raised the cry of 'religion in danger' to excite and mislead the ignorant. Thus Malabari and his lieutenants had, not only the apathy of an alien government to overcome, but also the active antipathy and opposition of his reactionary countrymen themselves. These latter tried to frighten Government by conjuring up pictures of another mutiny, which would follow its interference in social matters. For months were rebellions and civil wars wildly talked about, as the inevitable result of this social reform movement. But Malabari anticipated every move of that kind, and foiled its tactics at every turn.

After six years' preparation and organization in India itself, he thought of enlisting directly the sympathy of the people, and especially the women, of England, on his side. His question being a women's question, he judged rightly that it would be helped forward by English women. He knew the immense power that English women have learnt to wield. He determined to utilize this power in putting the machinery of the State in motion. Personal interviews were his chief instruments here. He went to England thrice on this mission. He addressed an eloquent and pathetic 'Appeal' to the 'women of England,' on behalf of their Indian sisters. He interested the whole English press in the subject in a manner unknown before. He also tackled opponents in high position and won them over to his side. Mr. Herbert Spencer may be said to be one of these converts to Malabari's theory of the necessity of State aid in dealing with what he calls 'certain outer aspects of social reform.' Finally, a committee, consisting of the most influential and representative persons, including prominent English as well as Anglo-Indian statesmen, men of letters and philanthropists, was established in London, to urge the necessity of legislative action on the Indian Government. The chief recommendation, formally submitted by this committee, was to raise by law the minimum of the girl's age when a marriage can be consummated from ten to twelve years. This was embodied in the famous Age of Consent Bill of 1891, passed by the Government of Lord Lansdowne. The English friends who co-operated with Malabari were very zealous in the cause ; in fact, they were too zealous for him in some respects. They were not content with his mild proposals. If they had their own way, they would have forced the Indian Government to go much further in this matter of social reform than it would have liked to go. But Malabari impressed upon them the prime necessity of hastening slowly. He sometimes found it more difficult to control his war-horses than to rouse them to action. Thus the man who was denounced by the reactionaries in India as a firebrand, was the very man who saved the reform movement from proceeding at too rapid and headlong a rate. It is well known that throughout his crusade Malabari has refused to act as a professional agitator, to embarrass or stultify Government, even when smarting under their slowness to move.

The Age of Consent Act, which raised the age from

ten to twelve, may appear to the English to be a trivial advance. Even twelve, they may contend, is not at all adequate for the purpose, and must be raised at least to fourteen. But for India the advance must be considered a great and beneficent achievement. Hereafter the age will doubtless be raised to fourteen, and probably to sixteen. The people themselves, after experiencing the benefits of the present Act, may desire such a rise. The Act will thus have an educative influence. But even as it is, it will do immense good. The years between ten and twelve constitute the most critical period in the development of an Indian girl; and her protection during this period is an inestimable gain. The years between twelve and fourteen are considered less critical for the Indian wife than between ten and twelve. This was one reason why a comparatively low limit was accepted. The measure is also recognized as a vindication of a grand principle, namely, that nothing, not even custom or religion itself, shall be allowed to militate against the interests of humanity. The Age of Consent Act is the result of Malabari's advocacy of social reform in England as well as India, during nearly ten years, supported by the patriotic zeal and learning of his friend, Mr. Dayaram Gidumal; and he may well be proud of it. If true greatness is to be measured, not so much by the greatness of the result achieved as by the magnitude of the difficulties overcome, and of the obstacles removed during the effort, then the leader of Indian Social Reform must be said to be really a great man. His efforts show what could be achieved by single-minded zeal and perseverance. Even after the passing of this Act he has not been idle. He is busy urging the Government to take up the second proposal of the committee in London, that about abolishing the English-imported law regarding the 'restitution of conjugal rights.' His work, moreover, is not limited to public exertions like those we have recorded. His private efforts for social reform are indefatigable. He has working committees in almost every part of the country, which help, personally, with money and influence, those who are in need of support. Malabari and his committees are not content with talking and passing resolutions as to the desirableness of the remarriage of widows and other such questions. They try actually to bring about these improvements by means of persuasion and pecuniary aid. They also employ social reform preachers, whose business is to travel about and show the better way to the people. Malabari is in regular correspondence with his agents, as to every little act of benevolence, and opens his purse as freely as he wields his pen.

CHAPTER VIII.

WITH the passing of the Age of Consent Act his active career seems to have closed, for the present at least. His all-engrossing, self-imposed task is over. And like most active men, he repines at this loss of occupation. He seems never to be at his ease but when engrossed with some work for the good of his fellow-men. He is young, being barely forty-one, though in these forty-one years he has done more than a single life's work. He may still undertake another great cause of reform, and devote his maturer energies to it.

Malabari visited England thrice, though for a short while only each time. His visits were connected with the question of social reform, and he was really engrossed in his work of conversion. But still he was never so busy as to allow his powers of observing and studying human nature and character to lie idle. And in England he had a very wide and novel field. He utilized his unusual opportunities of observing English life in several grades, and made notes of the more striking features. These he has worked out in his recently published book, entitled *The Indian Eye*

† K 2

on English Life. In this volume he does for his own countrymen, as regards England, what he has already done for Englishmen about Gujarat. The work is almost entirely critical, though there are also some extremely vivid and lifelike descriptions of men and things. The criticism is not always favourable to the people observed and criticized; in some places it is severely adverse. Yet the whole book is conceived in such a candid spirit, the critic is so generous, so anxious to give credit for everything that he could honestly praise, and so singularly free is he from prejudices, that few will be inclined to find fault with him even when differing from his views. In this book we see English life at home and in public analyzed with rare tact and judgement. The Englishman may see himself in it as an acute foreigner of wide sympathies and true culture sees him, and may profit by this very kindly light vouchsafed to him. As might be expected, the book has run through three editions in a year. The first edition was received with warm applause by the leading journals in England, India, and even in France. In this last country, too, the book is likely to become popular, if translated by a sympathetic hand. The French are very curious to know all about English character, and their literature contains two excellent works on it. Voltaire's *Lettres* depict, with the cynicism of that scoffer, the lighter aspects which the people of England present to an intelligent and observant foreigner. M. Taine's estimate is based on wider and more accurate observation, and therefore goes deeper. But both these French critics lack the wide sympathy and keen insight of the Indian, which have made his criticisms juster as well as more profound, and yet more palatable. As a literary work, the book is allowed to possess merits of a very high order. It is replete with humour of that gentle, delicate kind which never hurts. The style is simple, lucid, and forcible, while here and there may be found passages of rare power and beauty, as the one, for instance, on Faith and Doubt. But with all its merits, the work is not comprehensive enough, omitting some important sides of English life. It also suffers, like much of his literary work, from want of method and of leisure. These blemishes, in fact, characterize the artist as well as his work. He seems to be always in a hurry, and his work bears distinct traces of this. He suggests more than he explains. This is due partly to defects of early training, and more so to the literary artist having merged himself in the practical philanthropist. Be this what it may, the *Indian Eye* is remarkably free from the crudities of some of his earlier writings. A Saturday Reviewer compares the author of the *Indian Eye* with Mr. Rudyard Kipling at his best, whilst other critics have welcomed the book in terms of high praise, expecting from it nothing but good both to England and to India. This is really the tendency of almost everything that Malabari has written. His *Indian Muse* and *Gujarat and the Gujaratis* are instances in point. If some enterprising publisher were to bring out a handy reprint of these writings, with some of those autobiographical sketches scattered over the columns of the *Indian Spectator*, we believe he would confer a lasting benefit on the public, while at the same time making a good investment for himself. A volume or two of Malabariana would be appreciated all over the world where the English language is spoken. His English and vernacular works might also be placed with advantage within the reach of the student class. Not a few of them deserve to be used as text-books at school and college.

Malabari's latest literary work is a small volume of verse, put forth under the title of *Anubhavika*, that is, 'Experiences in Life.' In it he returns to mother Gujarati, as in his earliest poetical effort, and gives a series of sonnets, moralizing on some of the strange and almost dramatic experiences he has obtained in life. A high ethical tone predominates here, as in all his poetical works. The poem on Active Duty is one of the best in the volume. The volume contains an introductory ode to his native Gujarat, which shows the deep love he still cherishes for the country of his birth and early training. He has seen, over and over again, the whole continent of India ; indeed, there are very few who know it so well as he. He has seen England and English life. He has seen Europe. Yet his heart, like a true patriot's, yearns for his beloved province of Gujarat, where were laid the scenes of his childhood. This is characteristic of him. Though he has imbibed the true spirit of Western civilization and culture, he does not despise the East, and loves the land of his birth with an undying love.

We must not omit some mention here of *The Indian*

Problem, published in the shape of a memorandum
during his third visit to England. In this Malabari
gave, in his own forcible and felicitous language, the
gist of a conversation he had had with certain leading
statesmen. The leaflet takes an all-round view of the
present political situation in India ; explains how the
difficulties of governing it will increase with the increase of English education and the spread of Western
ideas ; to what extent the difference in ideals is
responsible for the growing tension between natives
and Europeans ; and what are the real dangers ahead,
as distinct from the imaginary. With charming frankness he ' preaches at' the official class, on the one
hand, and at their critics in the press, on the other.
All this he does without indulging in one offensive
remark in the course of his discussion of some of the
most bitterly controverted topics of the day. He
must be a true friend of India and England alike who
dares so much for each of them. Owing to its own
merits, no less than the position of the writer, *The
Indian Problem* is looked upon as a sort of *vade
mecum* for statesmen and publicists. It has had the
general approval of responsible officers of the Crown
and leaders of opinion.

We have now rapidly glanced at Malabari's work,
literary and philanthropic. Within our narrow limits
we have not had enough space for personal details.
To describe the work, rather than the personality of
the hero, has been our object, and consistently with it
we have hitherto spoken almost entirely of Malabari's
work. This is also in keeping with his own aim in

life. He has sunk his personality in his work and his cause. Complete effacement of self has been his ideal; and he has steadily pursued it throughout his later life. This is not because he is without ambition. Naturally, he says, he is very ambitious, fully sharing that last failing of noble minds. But, by a course of severe self-discipline, he has crushed all personal ambition and love of self out of himself. In this alone, if not in other respects, his life is a great lesson to those who would do good to their country. Public life is affected chiefly from ambitious motives and love of fame. Popular applause, the admiration of gazing multitudes, is as the very breath of the nostrils to most public men. Malabari has steadily avoided such popularity. Nor has he ever cared for a life of ease and comfort. For a man of his opportunities, he has preferred to live in poverty and obscurity, without noise or show of any kind, except such as the nature of his work rendered unavoidable. It is an open secret that he has spent the larger half of his income on public objects ever since he began to earn. Talking to him one day on the subject, the present writer asked how he could give so much and so often from his little, and yet manage to live so well. What could this mean? His answer was characteristic: 'Shall I tell you what it means? It means the same coat to your back for years, the same everything else so long as you could pull on with it. It means no carriage, no living in style, no going out into society. It sometimes means being very nearly run over by an upstart's carriage, said upstart cracking his whip behind you. In some matters, it means daily, hourly self-denial. But I do not repine. What was perhaps a trial, at first, has now become something like a triumph.'

We have seen how in the prime of manhood, at the very height of popularity, with the applause of the multitude as if ringing in his ears, he bethought himself of the dreams of duty that had haunted him in his boyhood's day: how he descended, as it were, from the crest of the wave, to wander barefooted over the thorny path of poverty and obloquy; how he declined all honours and profits, shutting his eyes, not only to his own future, but even to that of his children, arguing, ' if they share the privileges of my life, they must share its privations too.' Henceforth he has lived only for others. Many have profited by his advice and help— from the Raja or Rani in trouble to the school-girl in Europe struggling with religious doubt, or the Indian school-boy at home or abroad struggling with poverty. Many have been helped by him to official or social position. And some of these have abused his kindness, betrayed his confidence, traded upon his name, even personated the unsuspecting recluse for their own evil purposes. But no abuse or ill-requital has turned him against his fellows. His 'enthusiasm of humanity' has remained unabated in spite of all difficulties and disappointments. It was probably this trait in his character that once reminded a distinguished civilian of the career of that prince of enthusiasts, Gautama Buddha.

It required no ordinary self-denial in a man of his

talents and inclinations to keep himself out of the
sphere of active politics wherein, chiefly, educated
Indians are assured of public applause. He has kept
out of the reach of all such applause. He chose his
own quiet way of public usefulness, and has persevered
in his choice through good report and evil. The name
and fame he has achieved have come rather in spite
of his efforts than owing to them. Had he chosen to
become a political force, there is no saying how high
this 'born leader of men,' as Colonel Olcott has
described him, might have risen. Had he chosen to
shine as a literary star, he could have occupied perhaps
the largest space in the galaxy of letters. But early
in life he realized the urgent need of championing the
cause of social reform, that is the cause of the weak
and the neglected, and he determined to do this
himself. How well he has done it we have seen in
the preceding pages. He has given up a brilliant
career, given up all ambition, as has been observed by
Professor Max Müller, many cherished friendships, nay,
health itself and peace of mind, in order to serve his
cause. He has had to fight against long-established
usage and prejudice, not only in his own province, but
all over the continent. But he has succeeded in carrying out a considerable part of his programme in spite
of staggering obstacles and opposition at almost every
step. Naturally, he has made enemies on many sides,
though he has never acted like a firebrand, nor acted,
Ishmael-like, with his hand against every one and
every one's hand against him. His prudence and
moderation have led him always to proceed on the

lines of least resistance, and to make as few opponents as possible. But still, his efforts to reform Hindu society have shocked conservative minds, and all these have not yet had the generosity to forgive him. But if they could not find it in their hearts to forgive Malabari, *he* has forgiven them all. Few know what wrongs he has forgiven, in his private as well as public dealings. If he is great in his power of giving, he is even greater in his power of forgiving. His opponents have sometimes gone out of their way to question his motives, charging him with selfishness and love of notoriety. That a man, who resolutely set his face against self-aggrandizement, who declined offer after offer of friendly aid, who has avoided every form of recognition from the State and from society; that a man who leads the simple ascetic life that Malabari leads, shunning the world, despising all its pleasures, and owning nothing beyond a bare competence, earned by the sweat of his brow and the force of his pen; that such a man should be charged with interested motives, shows the straits to which his opponents must have been reduced, for want of facts and arguments. Whatever may be his faults—and he has never sought to conceal these—selfishness and love of the world are certainly not among them. If he had looked to self, and had swerved from the path of rectitude but a little, he would not have remained to-day the poor man that he is. He is sometimes stigmatized as a friend of the official class, whom he is supposed to keep in good humour. But if the truth were known, the relations between Malabari and his official friends would be found to be entirely to his credit. As we have observed, he is beholden to none of them. If anything, the balance lies in his favour, so far as good offices and friendly counsel go, in the interest of the public and the Government, which he has always held to be identical. On the other hand, the officials find in him, when they are in the wrong, an unsparing critic. By means of his paper, and still more by means of private correspondence with the authorities, he has tried hard to expose the irregularities of individual officials, some of whom have thus come to hate him and discredit his public movements.

But it is always the fate of such characters to be misunderstood or underrated in their lifetime. They themselves, however, care little for it. They find sufficient consolation in the consciousness of doing good. The consciousness of having a high ideal, and of their efforts to attain that, cheers up such noble natures. It is conducive to the good of the world around them to know and appreciate them. It is always refreshing and edifying to find, in the midst of thousands pursuing commonplace worldly objects, a few soaring above them, following a lofty ideal and giving up all that the rest consider so vitally important in this pursuit. The world is not so ignorant nor perverse as to refuse to appreciate a great character when it is shown one. Still his contemporaries are too near and know too little of him to understand Malabari thoroughly. For that the due perspective of time is required. Posterity can do better justice to great men. So when the present generation shall have passed away, and the succeeding ones shall come to cast up a proper account of its deeds and to estimate the men who did them, who shall reap the harvest of the laborious lives now spent for their benefit; when many of the names that now loom so large or figure so often before the public shall shrink to their due significance; when, in short, every deed and every man shall appear in their true proportions; it may confidently be predicted that the name of Behramji Malabari—poet, philosopher and publicist, the true national reformer, the champion of the rights of child-wives and child-widows—shall be remembered as that of the greatest benefactor of India in his day, and the warmest friend of England. Then shall it be time to realize that it is possible for one to discard all personal ambition, and to make one's life sublime by the exercise of incessant and uncomplaining self-sacrifice.

SUPPLEMENT

THE writer of this sketch is indebted to several of Mr. Malabari's friends, who have been good enough to help him with their impressions of the man and his work. Of these, the following extracts from the letters of the Countess of Jersey, Sir John Scott, Sir William Wedderburn, and last, but not least, Mr. Ardasir Framji, perhaps the most cultured Parsi gentleman, and father of our first lady graduates, will be read with special interest :—

FROM THE COUNTESS OF JERSEY.

. . . What most impressed me was the singular absence of desire on his part to acquire for himself any advantage or notoriety in the course of his efforts for his country's good. Many prominent people in London society would gladly have received Mr. Malabari as an honoured guest; others would willingly have raised subscriptions for the furtherance of his work. Mr. Malabari, however, declined both personal recognition and pecuniary aid. All that he desired was sympathy and assistance in forcing certain social evils on the notice of those who might influence public opinion. I do not know when I have met with a man so single and devoted in his aim. I hope that your account of this philanthropist will prove useful and stimulating to your readers.

FROM SIR JOHN SCOTT.

. . . Mr. Malabari is, in the truest sense, a reformer, not a mere innovator. His keen interest in politics has not blinded him to the fact that social reform must precede political reform, or, at any rate, is of greater importance. The homes and inner life of the people must be made healthy, morally and physically, before any solid improvement of the outer life is attempted. Infant marriages and enforced widow-hood of infant wives are far greater blocks to the political develop-ment of India than any of her Congressmen imagine. Indeed, the whole treatment of women as inferiors, needing no genuine education and having no real equality, is fatal to progress. This was realized by Mr. Malabari, and he set himself to social reform as the one big task of his life ; and his earnest, eloquent crusade has had the success it deserved. He is, too, a writer of a rare kind, for he has originality and earnestness, whether he writes on Gujarat or London. His grasp of political problems is noteworthy, and his power of seeing all sides gives him that moderation which convinces.

From Sir William Wedderburn.

. . . I am glad that you are intending to write an account of Mr. Malabari's career, as an example to his countrymen of philan-thropic self-sacrifice. I have had Mr. Malabari's friendship for many years, and have watched with admiration his great and untiring energy in the cause of suffering humanity, his sympathy being strongest for those who are most helpless. In ancient times, those who desired to convert the people had to depend upon oral teaching. Such oral teaching Mr. Malabari has carried on systematically, travelling about as a social missionary. But modern times have, in addition, given him the power of the press ; and by means of his journal and other publications he has preached his doctrines over the length and breadth of India. I shall rejoice if you can stimulate the younger generation to follow him in his self-denying labours for the social welfare of the whole Indian community.

From Mr. Ardasir Framji.

. . . I have known Mr. Malabari for the last twenty years, and have watched the growth of his mind and of his work. He is such an intimate friend of mine, and has filled such a large place in my thoughts and in my respect, that it would be difficult, when speaking of him, to prevent myself from falling into exaggeration. His life has been to me a subject of speculation as to the possibility of develop-ment of the highest order, apart from educational influences.

The main features of his character are a high emotion and a keen intellect; but such is the predominance of the former that the latter is content to be entirely in its service. No one, not intimate with him, can know to what a multitude of interests he is always prepared to devote himself, provided they concern the relief of human misery or wrong; and his capacity in this respect, when he took up the cause of nearly the entire womanhood of this country, has been known to all. He is happiest when thus engaged. The energy which he then exhibits, the journeys àcross country he undertakes, the pecuniary sacrifices he makes, the voluminous correspondence he engages in, and the writings he pours out, are a matter of wonder. On the other hand, any lull in such work makes him restless, moody, and melancholy. It is this which has led him to look upon such work as his destined vocation, for Mr. Malabari is a firm believer, in a broad way, in Divine providence actively though inscrutably at work in this world.

As to the keenness of his intellect, the proof lies broadcast in his writings. His unique mastery, from the moment he entered upon public life, over the English language, such as few, if any, natives of this country have attained, is all the more inexplicable, remembering that he is not an *alumnus* of any of our colleges, and is not at all a man of books. His mastery of pure Gujarati is equally remarkable, and I have been often set a-thinking, with the example of our friend before me, whether it may not be possible to find out the secret of mental constitution which enables a person to arrive, by an infinitely shorter route than the educational machinery in vogue supplies, to some of the highest mental attainments. It is not simply the facility of expression that I am referring to, but also what I have come to consider as the intuitive grasp of the most salient points of the questions which come before him. He goes straight to the heart of a subject. It is, I am sure, mainly to the effective service of his intellect, through the medium of the English language, that he owes the success he has obtained as out and out the foremost of our social reformers. To that success a combination of other qualities has also helped, namely, a strong common sense, enabling him to arrange and manage his *modus operandi*; self-humility, which makes him keep himself in the background and put forth no claim to recognition; a happy vein of humour, which, in union with a sympathetic nature, prevents his efforts from degenerating into mere censoriousness, and which, at times, is only next door to pathos, the incongruity provoking the humour leading him straight to a pathetic estimate of the situation, never to scorn; a spirit of self-sacrifice, which confines his personal expenses within rigorous bounds, only the better to enable him to relieve distress and further any good cause; and a simplicity which scorns self-indulgence or self-pampering of every kind, and confines him to the most simple fare, the most simple, not to say coarse dress, and the most simple house conveniences, his bedding being but a thin mattress stretched upon a rudimentary bedstead devised by himself, or upon the bare floor.

And now for the highest trait in the character of our friend. It is the habitual, though by no means painless, suppression of the lower before the higher nature, the enforced subjection of selfish desires to the rule of right conduct from a sense of duty. It was from the date of a crisis in his life, which resulted in the victory of his higher nature, that I have watched the steady growth of his spiritual and intellectual nature, the maturity of which is now apparent to all who have the benefit of his intimacy. He gives bountifully from his slender store; has declined a fortune, honours, titles, and worldly position. He has been for years the trusted referee of men of the highest positions, in and out of the country, on questions of moment and delicacy; and his mediation has been sought for or accepted in emergencies of grave misunderstanding or difference between the rulers and the ruled. Dreading all ceremony and the pomp and circumstance of riches, he loves to associate with the poor and the lowly-minded, and would sooner be at the bedside of the sick and the dying than at a wedding or a pleasure party. Our friend is tenderhearted and humble-minded, though by no means careless of the esteem of others. I have seen him take home a forsaken dog from the street and adopt him, pay the ancestral debts of a poor honest servant, and rise from his seat and reach out a stool to a clumsy servant to stand on when lighting a lamp. People, high and low, call upon him on affairs public and private. He never spares himself, but when unable to stand the strain retires to a suburban place, to which, of course, he is soon tracked. You should see what he amusingly calls his office. It is a dingy little place, an *otla* (veranda), ten by six, with two old chairs, a narrow old writing-desk and bare floor. Here people come to see him, from the helpless widow, the bearer of a begging-letter, to the High Court Judge or Member of Council, the Indian Raja or the British Peer.

It would be no disparagement of such a character to say, as the fact is, that he is not a man of society or of sociable habits. He is reserved and sometimes moody, and is preoccupied before strangers. He is so shy that he will not get into a carriage of any pretension unless the hood is up or it is dark. At times he is sorely puzzled with a world not moving to his mind. All this is but the penalty of an excessive sensibility. He is conscious of these defects, and blames himself for being unable to get the better of them. For all this, Mr. Malabari has.the grip of a Howard or a Wilberforce, his literary performances apart.

I must not omit one more peculiarity. My friend sometimes goes out with his family for a change. He then takes with him a colony of connexions, not omitting an acquaintance or two into the bargain. He wants to be alone and recruit himself, you see! But, then, what right has he to prefer himself to others? He pays a tremendous bill, caring not to look into it. Such is the man!

INDEX

OXFORD : HORACE HART,
PRINTER TO THE UNIVERSITY

CARLYLE'S UNPUBLISHED LECTURES

ON

EUROPEAN LITERATURE AND CULTURE.

Edited by Mr. R. P. KARKARIA, B.A.

•

————◆◆————

'Mr. Karkaria's extremely able Introduction brings before us with admirable lucidity the two opinions which are the guiding lines of these lectures, the necessity of belief for true progress and culture, and the "well-known view that all great things are unconscious".'—*Guardian*, London, 1892.

'In the last lecture there is much true Carlyle. When he writes of Goethe, one feels at once that the main subject is his own, and that he instructs out of the fulness of knowledge. Two theories distinctly run and connect the course of lectures, and we cannot do better than quote these lines from the Introduction of Mr. Karkaria.'—*Spectator*, London, 1892.

'But for Mr. Karkaria's industry these lectures would still be lying submerged among the dingy records of the Bombay Asiatic Society. . . It is a notable mark of Mr. Karkaria's triumph over the characteristic touches, not of mere idiom but of literary instinct which they reveal, and of the intrinsic soul of sympathy with which he edits his work, that it would puzzle the wariest critic to discern wherein his style and the direction of his thought are distinguishable from British standards.'— *Catholic Examiner*, Bombay, 1892.

'Of the two simultaneous first publications of what Mr. R. P. Karkaria calls Carlyle's posthumous work, we prefer that which this gentleman has himself edited. . . It is also to Mr. Karkaria's credit as an editor that he leaves his reader in no doubt as to the real character and authenticity of those lectures.'—*St. James's Gazette.*

'We now come to Mr. Karkaria's Introduction, which is admirably written in a modest, sympathetic and scholarly fashion. . . As a rule the editorial work is most carefully done.'—*Times of India*, 1892.

'Mr. Karkaria has done his work as editor with an ability and good taste which prove that he thoroughly deserved his good fortune in making the find. The lectures in themselves are well worth reading, not only for their clearness and the wonderful way in which the perspective is preserved, but also for their interest in giving, in a more or less colloquial form, the first rough hewings of some opinions which afterwards shaped into inimitable Carlylese, roused controversies not yet stilled.'—*Bombay Educational Record.*

'When Carlyle gets upon ground with which he is more familiar—that of the literary history of the modern world—his native genius reappears here and there. In what he says about Dante and his age, about Luther and the Reformation, about Cervantes and chivalry, about the literature of the *Aufklärung*, about Swift, Johnson, Hume, and Gibbon, and finally about Goethe and his influence, we seem once more to catch vivid glimpses of Carlyle whom we know and admire. . . The notes of Mr. Karkaria are less pretentious and often more to the point than those of Professor Greene.'—*Times*, London.

'The Bombay book has the advantage of much more elaborate editing than has been vouchsafed to the London one. Mr. Karkaria has taken the trouble to add a number of notes, interesting in themselves, and calculated to elucidate the text. So much is there of racy insight and imaginative language in these lectures, and so magical is the general charm of Carlyle's genius, that we read them to the last word, and then regretted that they were at an end.'—*Literary World.*

'They serve to give us as much insight into Carlyle's own culture, and his wide acquaintance with literature at the middle period of his life. His observations are fresher, and these are particularly interesting. Mr. Karkaria's text is taken from Anstey's original MS. The editor has been so painstaking in identifying Carlyle's references and in quoting parallel or similar passages from his own or others writings, that it would be ungracious to find fault with the naïve criticisms on which he occasionally ventures.'—*Athenaeum*, London.

'The most important point is that Mr. Karkaria has verified the countless references made by Carlyle, and gives in footnotes valuable parallel passages and quotations, sometimes cited by Carlyle and sometimes supplied by himself. The Introduction is careful and scholarly.'—*Bookseller*, London.

Mr. Malabari's Literary Works

To be had at the *Voice of India* Office, Bombay.

Proceeds to be devoted to Social Reform.

.

NITI-VINOD.—GUJARÁTI.

Second Edition.

(*Extracts from some Press opinions.*)

' To infuse into the Eastern mind something of the lofty tone of thought and feeling which distinguishes the most approved literary productions of the West, is what the clever young author has attempted in these pages. . . They evince considerable originality and reflect a lofty tone of moral teaching.'—*Times of India*, 1875 and 1876.

' Evidence of the mastery which even Parsis can acquire over a language, which they have either been too idle or too unfitted by nature to adopt, after vainly striving to do so for twelve centuries.'—*Indian Statesman*, 1875.

' The plan and execution of the work are original and bold.'—*Bombay Gazette*, 1876.

' There has been no genuine poet amongst the Parsis up to this time. .. A number of small but sweet and beautiful verses on various interesting subjects.'—*Rast Goftar*, 1875.

' The different metres seem to us to be faultless in their construction ; and most of the lines smooth and graceful. . . Some passages are really of the highest order. . . In other lines the author displays the powers of a painter.'—*Vidya Mitra*, 1875.

THE INDIAN MUSE IN ENGLISH GARB, AND OTHER ENGLISH VERSES.

' My Dear Sir,

I return my best thanks for your *Indian Muse in English Garb.* It is interesting, and more than interesting, to see how well you have managed in your English garb.

I wish I could read the poems which you have written in your own vernacular ; for, I doubt not they deserve all the praise bestowed upon them by the papers.

Believe me, your far-away but sincere friend,

1878.   A. Tennyson.'

'Depend upon it, the English public, at least the better part of it, likes a man who is what he is. The very secret of the excellence of English literature lies in the independence, the originality and truthfulness of English writers. . . In the verses where you feel and speak like a true Indian you seem to me to speak most like a true poet. Accept my best thanks and good wishes, and believe me,

Yours sincerely,

1878.   F. MAX MÜLLER.'

' " To the Missionaries of Faith," with its appended note,—the note on Zoroaster, p. 94—I have read with the greatest interest. . . The " Sketch" or Memoir is very striking ; so are the "Stages of a Hindu Female Life." . . May God bless your labours! May the Eternal Father bless India, bless England, and bring us together as one family, doing each other good. May the fire of His love, the sunshine of His countenance, inspire us all !

1878.   FLORENCE NIGHTINGALE.'

'You have such a cloud of witnesses to the excellence of the work, the high character of its poetry and its sentiments, and to the proof of singular ability, in such a mastery by a Foreigner, of the English language, that any favourable opinion of mine would be but a drop in the ocean.

1879.   SHAFTESBURY.'

'Your lines to Wordsworth prove that you have found your way into the secret of perhaps the deepest poetic influence of this century, and I rejoice to learn that his profound teachings thus make their way into wholly new modes of thought and feeling with penetrating sympathy.

1878.   J. ESTLIN CARPENTER.'

' It is a gratification to myself, which I cannot forego, to hail the appearance of a true poet and master-mind in India.

1880.   EDWARD B. EASTWICK.'

'A gifted young Parsee. The sonnets were written in memory of the late Princess Alice, and breathe a pathos and sympathy very warm and deep. There are, we think, some indications in it of the immaturity of the writer's powers; but we cannot but admire the noble picture he has drawn of what seems to be his ideal of womanly excellence.'—*Bombay Gazette,* 1879.

'Mr. Malabari appears to be a man of great individuality of character and talent, and endowed with keen poetical instincts.'—*Madras Athenaeum and Daily News,* 1879.

'The letter Mr. Malabari received from the Princess Alice in acknowledge-
ment of his work had such an effect on him, that on the recent death of
that amiable and accomplished lady, he embalmed her memory in a
trinity of beautiful English sonnets. A copy of the sonnets forwarded to
H.M. the Queen has elicited two warm messages of thanks and appreciation. . . This is a great compliment to the poet's genius and character.'—
Calcutta Statesman, 1879.

'Possesses considerable original power. It would be hard to over-
estimate the difficulties which throng around the native writer who
endeavours to adapt his thoughts to the rigid and circumscribed require-
ments of English prosody, with its poverty in rhymes, and all the refined
niceties of its metrical forms, which, while they help real genius, are
stumbling-stones in the path of the ungifted. In his poetical tribute to
the memory of the Princess Alice, our poet has poured his thoughts into
the daintiest, as it is the most artificial, of all our lyrical moulds.'—
Madras Mail, 1879.

'The writer has succeeded in drawing, in eloquent English verse, a very
fine picture of England's popular Princess. Mr. Malabari seems to be
a born poet. . . He also takes keen interest in the moral and social
progress of his countrymen; and his earnest and manly endeavours in
that direction, as also in faithfully interpreting the relations of India to
England, ought to be appreciated by both countries. Such men are all
too few in this country.'—*Englishman,* 1879.

'His poems prove that he is animated by noble aspirations, and that
he has a desire to discriminate truly between what is worthy and unworthy in life, and a power of enthusiastic admiration and friendship. . .
What he writes has a genuine character. His command of the language
is wonderful, and there are probably few poems written by an Indian
equal to those before us.'—*Journal of the National Indian Association,*
1878.

'His command over the English language is simply incredible, and we
can personally testify to his high intelligence, disinterested patriotism and
unselfish devotion.'—*Amrita Bazar Patrika,* 1878.

WILSON-VIRAH.—GUJARÁTI.

'The language of *Wilson-Virah* is simpler and more racy than of *Niti-
Vinod*; and its original thoughts, descriptive power and genuine poetic
expression reflect credit on the author's genius.'—*Jam-e-Jamshed,* 1878.

'His readers are not only loving Parsis, but admiring Hindus. And
no wonder. For Mr. Malabari's language is not only pure, it is the
purest of the pure. . . But when we read his noble sentiments and his
keen appreciation of Nature, it certainly makes us think very highly of
him. Even his prose partakes of the nature of poetry.'—*Gujarat Mitra,*
1878.

'As a divine, *savant*, and philanthropist, the poet describes his hero in eulogistic terms, but in artistic style. The lines evince great mastery of language. . . The language is melodious, and the narrative is enriched . with similes, metaphors, and other poetic characteristics.'—*Indian Daily News*, 1878.

SAROD-I-ETTEFÁK.—GUJARÁTI.

'The best harmony and the best poetical spirit. . . When it is seen that many of these verses were written some fifteen years ago, it will be granted that Mr. Malabari was born with all the powers of a first-rate poet. The fire of Religion, the aspirations of Love, the strengthening of Virtue, the yearning after Friendship, and contempt of this false World . . . these subjects have been treated in spontaneous language and in metres that could be rendered into music. . . What heart will not overflow with enthusiasm and delight by a perusal of the dramatic romance, "Pákdáman" (Lady Chastity) and "Shah Nargesh" (Prince Narcissus)? . . . The lines on Fortune may adorn the musician's art and may breathe hope into those who are discontended with their lot. "Bioga Bilap" and "Prabbu Prarthna" will prove refreshing to two intoxicated souls—the love-intoxicated and the faith-intoxicated. . . These noble lines will work powerfully upon the singer as well as the hearer. . . In short, the highest forms of poetry abound in these verses, and they are sure to fascinate the student of Nature with their deep meditative spirit like that of Wordsworth or Milton.'—*The Gujaráti*, 1882.

'Some of the poems are as finished as a beautiful picture. . . Many of them, being songs, will be a cherished treasure to the lover of music. . . . The description beginning with page 11 is so life-like, that it excites terror; but the writer seems to have used consummate art in managing his language. . . The portrait of beauty is very pure and vivid. Almost all the pieces evince deep love of Nature and her Maker; whilst some of the verses hide such a depth of meaning as could be fathomed only by a reader gifted with poetic instincts. . . Manly dignity, grace and melody, these are the peculiar merits of our young poet. He writes with reckless freedom; but like a true poet, keeps within bounds. In the treatment of religious subjects he evinces an intensely devout and meditative spirit. There are faults too in the work—immaturity, haste and abrupt terminations.'—*Bombay Chronicle*, 1882.

'Though composed some fifteen years ago, and though "the dim pictures of my childhood's experiences," these verses display a poet's powers. . . We observe evidences of the writer's high powers at every step. . . Pleasing, appropriate and affecting. . . The delicacy of feeling essential to a poet is not hard to find in Mr. Malabari.'—*Dnyan Vardhak*.

GUJARÁT AND THE GUJARÁTIS.

Third Edition.

'Many bright descriptions of native home life and customs. The author writes English with remarkable ease. . . Mr. Malabari sketches boldly, and has a satirical pen. . . Apart from the entertainment which it furnishes, there is much to be learnt from his book regarding both the merits and demerits of our rule in Hindustan as seen from the native point of view.'—*Daily News*, London, 1883.

'Sparkling series of sketches of Indian men and manners. . . The different castes and races are described with a skill and a humour that never fail. The author unlifts the veil from several ugly spots in our Indian Empire, but without even a dash of ill-humour or race antagonism. . . . Out of his own moral consciousness he evolves a fund of humour and of fun ; he points out abuses by no means attributable to the English, and now and then shows up things which the rulers would do well to consider and take to heart. But the most striking thing about the book is the completeness with which Mr. Malabari sees through the English. The Marwari, the Bora, the Hajam, the Vaqil, he describes from the outside ; but the Englishman, whom he does *not* set to work to describe, he seems to enter into as if he had been born within the sound of Bow Bells.'—*Vanity Fair*, London, 1883.

'The remarks which he makes upon the relations of the two races are few but outspoken, and whether the reader agrees with them or not, he cannot disallow the complete honesty and ingenuousness of the author. . . . The book gives original ideas and vivid pictures of Indian native life, worthy of consideration. . . That Mr. Malabari expresses the genuine native opinion on certain questions there is no reason to doubt. His words might be read with advantage by Government officials, high and low, engaged in the immense work of administering the affairs of Hindustan.'—*Morning Post*, London, 1883.

'After the production of this book no one need say that Indians are reticent as to their social and domestic affairs, or in the least shy in expressing their opinion on their European governors. There is a charming frankness throughout the whole book which cannot fail to win the approbation of every reader ; and this is happily accompanied by a pleasing witticism which precludes all suspicion of ill-natured carping.'— *Overland Mail*, London, 1883.

'Mr. Malabari's English style is remarkably good, and seldom exhibits any want of ease. His book is of special interest as throwing some light on the real feeling of the natives with regard to their British rulers.'— *Daily Telegraph*, London, 1883.

'A Parsi writer, honourably known as a journalist of the advanced sort, publishes a collection of bright and readable sketches, whose notable point is their genuine humour. . . The sincerity which seems inseparable from the gift of humour is the best feature of the sketches. . . He possesses, already, an intimate knowledge of native life, and a keen insight which is not to be deceived by appearances.'

'It is from the light thrown on modern native life, by such writers as Mr. Behramji Malabari, that the vast gulf, which separates the sordid and degraded Hinduism of the present day from the antique type, can be justly appreciated. The author has no wish to exaggerate the gloomy shadows that fall over this part of his subject; but he is too honest and sound a literary artist to entirely omit them, and he deserves great credit for a moderate and yet unflinching tone of veracity.'—*Civil and Military Gazette*, Lahore, 1883.

'Evidently the production of a conscientious writer, who reproduces with charming simplicity and *naïveté* such thoughts and ideas as suggest themselves to his mind.'—*Westminster Review*, London, 1883.

'With singular tact, and a ready flow of wit, he passes in review the chief people in the country, and analyses their actions and characters with considerable freedom. . . A vein of irony runs through the book, which is especially apparent when discussing modern improvements.'—*Army and Navy Magazine*, London, 1883.

'Mr. Malabari's pictures of men and manners in Gujarát have that greatest of all merits—the merit of being drawn from the point of view of a candid native. . . Altogether, the volume has somewhat the effect of an album of photographs, not always very pleasing, but, without exception, extremely real.'—*British Quarterly Review*, London, 1883.

'A carter speaks sweetly to his bullock, and we have no idea that the persuasive tones say, " Go on, bullock of my heart, go on, thy mother-in-law's darling ; " he takes to objurgations, and we cannot guess that he is shouting out, "Will you go on or not, you lazy widower, you son of a widow." . . The writer has powers of graphic description and a strong vein of humour. . . The life depicted is no high ideal, but one composed of many sordid materials, exposed in the book before us with an unsparing "photographic fidelity" which often reminds us of " Pandurang Hari".'—*Bombay Gazette*, 1883.

' " From grave to gay, from lively to severe : " there is scarcely any faculty of the mind which the writer of this work does not possess in a more or less eminent degree. . . The sketches of men and things Gujaráti, which form the bulk of the volume, are vivid life-pictures, full of humour and animation, as fresh as could be. . . Displays an extent of political insight and social and literary aptitude which no other single writer in India has yet displayed. . . His love of truth burns strong in almost every page, the feeling becomes almost a passion when the writer is "intense," to use his own word. Few English readers will be able to understand how the heart is being torn asunder by its intense suffering while the hand is busy mercilessly tearing up the veil from the face of vice, hypocrisy, and superstition, as exemplified by caste and its concomitant evils.'—*Indian Mirror*, Calcutta, 1883.

' The sufferings incident to child-marriage, the girl being older than the husband, are indicated in what is at once the most skilfully-drawn and curious episode in the work, entitled "An Aryan Idyll." . . The concluding passages of the "Aryan Idyll" are instinct with the truest pathos.'— *Allen's Indian Mail*, London, 1883.

' The same facility of word-painting, sly humour, and genuine liberality of view that characterised the book in its original form.'—*The Scotsman*, 1884.

' On the subject of these relations, Mr. Malabari discourses with notable penetration, candour, and impartiality. He acknowledges the great superiority of the British method of government over the preceding native *régimes* in respect of security and educational opportunities.'—*New York Sun*, 1884.

' While thus bantering in the tone he adopts when speaking of the tendency of some natives to earn cheap honours by toadying to their European superiors, Mr. Malabari is pitilessly stern in describing the shortcomings of native princes, especially if they happen to be of the type of Mulharao Guickowar. The spirit of the Indian reformer runs through the whole work.'—*Catholic Examiner*, 1884.

' As we read his descriptions of these characters, they seem to start into life and to walk before us. The barber particularly makes our flesh creep on our bones.'—*The Liberal*, 1884.

' A book in the pages of which we trace the master hand of a loving son of India. . . *Gujarát and the Gujarátis* is the very first book of its kind. It has the advantage of having a native for its author. . . There is scarcely a phase of the mind which is not exhibited in its pages, but the author throughout shows that he is the master, and never the slave, of his emotions.'—*The Hindu*, Madras, 1884.

' Written in a light and graceful manner and is replete with humorous touches. . . His views on public matters appear to be singularly enlightened.'—*Madras Mail*, 1884.

' The sketches given are vivid and picturesque, and are suffused with a vein of delicate humour which, set off in a clear, forcible style, clothes them with a peculiar interest. . . Another trait which characterizes the book is a spirit of benevolence and patriotism which runs through its pages.'—*Lahore Tribune*, 1884.

'It is written in a sprightly vein, and one is sometimes not certain if the author wishes to be taken seriously or not. . . This book is quite a gallery of pictures of the men in Western India who have any marked individuality.'—*Bombay Guardian,* 1884.

'A thousand times more valuable than those dry dissertations on the habits, character, and manners of the natives, with which the English reading public has been so long satisfied. The style of the book is lively, rollicking, and flexible, and reminds us in many places of Sir Ali Baba's happiest veins. The writter is truly a humorist in the best sense of the word. . . All these are graphic portraits with the unmistakable lineaments of truth, and tell us much more of native life than your bulky gazetteers and heavy books of travel. As for "week-day preaching," the volume before us contains many original observations, many incisive sayings, and many stirring exhortations.'—*Sindh Times,* 1884.

'Mr. Malabari's book is unique of his kind. It presents a picture of the different peoples of Gujarát, and of their different customs and habits ; and the tact and the literary skill used in describing them are such that they not only embellish the original subjects, but also serve, to a great extent, the purpose of a novel. His pictures are effective and humorous. . . . It is a century now since the British have been ruling over this country ; but they have not as yet acquired an adequate knowledge of the social customs and usages of the natives. Books like the one under review are, therefore, a help and a guide to Europeans in order to familiarize them with those customs and usages, and also to encourage social intercourse between them and the natives.'—*Bombay Samachar,* 1884.

'Mr. Malabari writes English not only well, but with humour, and picturesquely. . . The book is pleasant, spirited, and readable, with successful comic effects, introduced naturally and judiciously.'—*Cincinnati Gazette,* 1884.

'Its language is remarkable for its brilliant strokes, its vigour and pungency of style, and is very idiomatic—a little too much sometimes. . . Mr. Malabari is, above all, a poet.'—*Revue Critique,* 1884.

'In spite of Oriental solecisms, Mr. Malabari's English is, on the whole, powerful and easy, and has a quaintness which in many cases gives it a peculiar charm. . . It is obvious that Mr. Malabari has a real sense of humour, and some of his descriptions and incidents are laughable in the extreme. . . The refreshing candour of this account indicates one of the charms of the book. The same candour is displayed in all Mr. Malabari's sketches of Indian social and religious life.'—*Calcutta Review,* 1884.

'A writer of originality and power on the vital Indian questions of our day.'—SIR WILLIAM HUNTER, 1889.

'Through all the fearlessness of his denunciation of vices, his intense sympathy with the Hindu and Mahomedan population, no less than with his co-religionists, is never out of sight.   His perception of the defects of the rulers of the country does not blind him to their good qualities. . . The book teems with lessons for the European and the native, the ruler and the ruled, for the orthodox and conservative native, and the native reformer, sham or true, for the missionary, the statesman, the judge, the merchant, the British elector, and the Indian tax-payer.   It is a book that none but a native could have written, and no native but one with the special qualifications and great command of English possessed by the author.   His solecisms are few and far between, and tend only to add a picturesque ruggedness to his otherwise smoothly-rounded periods.'—*Madras Mail*, 1889.

'Mr. Malabari has much keen graphic power, and a strong sense of humour, sometimes amounting to sarcasm ; but the kindliness of his nature helps to qualify the occasional bitterness of his descriptions.   Few books on India throw such light, in a few words, on the ways and customs of the people.'—*Indian Magazine*, 1889.

THE INDIAN EYE ON ENGLISH LIFE.

Third Edition.

' Has a keenly observant eye and the gift of humour, and he gives his readers many vivid sketches of what he saw in the streets and houses of England. . . The author not only cleverly sketches the characters of others, but also reveals his own with the open-hearted candour of a Rousseau or a Cicero.'—*Bombay Gazette*, 1893.

'Intense originality and human interest. . . Every one remembers M. Taine's striking inference as to the respect felt for the English father from the fact that the young Englishman invariably speaks of him as " the Governor." Mr. Malabari, who might have been forgiven half a dozen flights of genius of this sort, has in that respect been happier than the illustrious author of *Letters from England*, so secure is he in a thoroughly idiomatic English, and is no stranger even to the English that is heard within sound of Bow Bells.   The book is, as we have said, decidedly original, and is strongly impressed with the personality of its author.   He manages—though it must have been a great effort to him—to keep his work as a social reformer in the background ; but, as in India he has been accustomed to see the State mainly in the home, so in England the home life of the people claims much more of his attention than our politics, our literature, or our intellectual life.   His observations are as a rule singularly correct. . .

' Like the *Athenaeum*, the *Saturday Review* has a long and highly appreciative notice of Mr. Malabari's new book.   The former thinks Mr. Malabari's account of English home life to be beautiful, and that Rudyard

Kipling himself has never done anything better than the narrative of the cheap-jack fleecing his customers outside the Crystal Palace. According to the *Saturday Review*, Mr. Malabari studies every branch of English life with the calm, modest, discriminating attention of one anxious to get at the truth on every occasion, and appreciate its bearings on the problems of Indian society. As regards the relations of Englishmen and Indians, Mr. Malabari, according to the *Review*, speaks with excellent good sense, good taste and dignity, and that such work could not fail to be of inestimable value, showing that on the gravest and most important topics the author is in close sympathy with all that is best among Englishmen. . .

'It is a hopeful sign of the times that the principal native papers of India appreciate the scope and object of Mr. Malabari's book on English life and manners. The *Hindu* of Madras, for example, has read the book with the greatest delight, and considers the author to be not only a philosopher, but also a true poet, albeit he writes in prose. The *Indian Mirror* of Calcutta, on the other hand, observes the same bright intelligence, penetration, sincerity of purpose, and independence, observable in this volume, which were so much admired in *Guzerat*, and which secured a European reputation for its author. Mr. Malabari's loyalty to truth is truly refreshing. . . But so kindly is his spirit of criticism that his victims, however much they may wince at first, will end by joining in the laugh against themselves. Looking at its varied contents, says the *Mirror*, this is a book for the reformer, the statesman, and the philanthropist.—*Times of India*, 1893.

'The London *Times* welcomes Mr. Malabari's *Indian Eye on English Life* as a remarkable volume of travels and experiences in England. It adds that Mr. Malabari understands our language perfectly, and writes it with a force and skill which many a native (English) writer might envy. He observes with a friendly, but not uncritical eye. . . In conclusion, the *Times* says that the book is in reality what Montesquieu's *Lettres Persanes* and other literary apologues only pretended to be. Mr. Malabari does not spare us, and sometimes his criticisms are, perhaps, a little captious. But he writes, on the whole, with a kindly pen, and gives us a rare opportunity of seeing ourselves as others see us.'—*Bombay Gazette*, 1893.

'Judged from his book, he seems to be a kindly philosopher; a man whose views have been mellowed, a man who thinks for himself, and is a keen observer of human nature. He combines the gentleness of "*le philosophe sous les toits*" of Emile Souvestre with the acute observation of Max O'Rell.'—*Indian Daily News*, 1894.

'The book is both shrewd and sympathetic—in fact, it does equal credit to the author's head and heart—and the tone of its comments and criticisms is happily neither ecstatic nor fulsome, but on the contrary, manly and frank.'—*The Speaker*, 1893.

'It will be seen that the author possesses no ordinary degree of susceptibility. He caught, as it were, the key of Venice, and unlocked the poetry of her canals in the course of a single evening! It is only, however, when he reaches London that we get the full benefit of all that Mr. Malabari's eye recorded and his imagination painted. On the whole he enjoyed himself, and thinks not unkindly of the land which has adopted him; but that does not prevent him from giving forth a great deal of interesting criticism.'—*The Englishman*, 1893.

'So much genuine perception of the strong points of European character, combined with such clear-sightedness in dealing with what we ourselves must admit to be very dark blots on English life. For European energy and organization the writer has unmixed praise, and he speaks with refreshing honesty. . . This abundance of life and energy, and yet withal of orderliness also, is, of course, the leading impression left on an Asiatic by a first sight of the streets of London. Another, which will also be familiar to many an Anglo-Indian on hard-earned furlough, is the number of women in those streets ; indeed the sex seems to have arrested the Indian eye from the first and (small wonder) to have claimed an almost unduly large share of attention. Observations on English women abound throughout the book, and those of us who are apt to resent any alien criticism on the fairer half of the people of England should be disarmed by the admiring sincerity with which it is expressed. .. Mr. Malabari is, as we all know, the most prominent leader in the cause of prevention of infant marriage, which he rightly regards as one of the most deleterious that can be named. But, he says, if he were asked to choose between drunkenness and that, he would keep to his own national custom. . . The parts of the book which deal with English home life and marriage are perhaps the best, and nowhere is the author's moderation and insight alike more apparent.'—*The Pioneer*, 1894.

'Mr. Malabari's book is drawing to itself much attention on the Continent. In a review in the *Journal des Débats* M. Augustin Filon attempts a very ingenious, and, upon the whole, accurate appreciation of the book, while at the same time he throws an interesting side-light on the personality of the author, whom he introduces as "A Grandson of Zoroaster." M. Filon may be himself recognised as guide, philosopher and friend to the late Prince Imperial, since whose death in Zululand he has preferred, like the Empress Eugenie, to live beyond the Channel, mixing with the best elements in English life. He may, therefore, be presumed to combine the critical appreciation of the English with the mother-wit of the French reviewer in estimating a book that has made no little stir in literary circles. . . "Gently but invincibly stubborn, at the same time pacific and combative, as behoves an apostle, Mr. Malabari has two languages, two countries, one of which conflicts with the other. Quite naturally, he loves that which suffers. He reasons and talks like an Englishman, but he feels like an Indian. He is one of those exceptional beings, in whom the conquered races become conscious of their defeat, by whom their decadence is arrested, by whom they are reinstated and put again on the path of progress. Very beautiful is the life of these men, but very bitter, very painful to live. Theirs are voices crying in the wilderness. They expiate every moment of their existence the fault of being born a century too soon ; and yet without them, this century to come, this century so much desired and so necessary, would not be born. Athens asked herself why she should obey Rome, and Rome, too, wondered at it herself, as she yielded to the conquered city the palm for superiority in art, beauty, and intellect. Verily, the relative situations of England and India are quite different. But it will be admitted that Mr. Malabari cherishes and venerates the Indian race, noble, refined and shrewd above all, the veritable aristocracy of nations, the mother and nurse of all civilizations. What are her weaknesses? Whereby has she merited her servitude? He knows it but too well. But this heavy and strong conqueror, who holds her in his claws ; how could he be known, how could the secret of his strength be found out except by going to and surprising him in his own country, in the midst of his own people, in that *home* of which he talks so much, and wherein he lives so little?" Here we have the origin of the volume, which strikes its French reviewer as being "really the book of a writer." To the English, its sentences may appear at times to be irregular and somewhat ill-balanced, "oscillating from the familiar, brutal, popular word to the most refined symbolism, at one time descending below prose, at another time rising to the height of true poetry." As for M. Filon, he admires the energy of thought, always at work, which creates for itself expression in a foreign and hostile tongue. " I admire it when it scoops, chisels, gives shape, and softens this rugged language, and expresses, in their shades and half-shades, its warmths and sorrows, its thousand and one delicate disquietudes, to which the English soul is an utter stranger. He forces the words to say that which they would not say, what they have never said, and besides, he invests them with that splendid imagery and colour which characterize the gorgeous East ".'—*Times of India*, 1894.

'A French critic has undertaken to wrestle with some of Mr. Malabari's " Reflections on English Civilization." This is M. G. Valbert, who devotes no fewer than thirteen pages of the *Revue des Deux Mondes* to a critical examination of the volume. . . Mr. Malabari, says his reviewer, loves his country passionately, but his love is clear-sighted. He is not blind to the weaknesses and miseries of a once noble race which has merited its present misfortunes ; and he has sworn to devote himself to its regeneration. He has too religious a soul to protest against the decree of fate that has handed India over to England. He is not prejudiced against the English, nor does he contest their superiority. He only criticises their methods of government, and blames them for being clumsy masters. He has no liking for the indulgent patrons who will neither force nor constrain, and whose smiles expresses good-will mixed with pity. Mr. Malabari believes he sees in this pity a little of contempt. . . M. Valbert sees "The Asiatic philosopher" surprised into a state of panic at sight of the mad rush of life in England—at the way in which the people eat, drink, talk, work, and amuse themselves. He pities their restlessness from the bottom of his heart, even as he admires their freedom and their independence. "Your life is a mad saraband," cries this wisest and most ironical of Parsis. But has the East found the real secret of human existence ? asks the West. Unrest is a mark of noble and progressive races—it is that which has made room for all inventions and discoveries, all beneficent reforms and innovations. We think it rather hard on Mr. Malabari to have to go to a French school to learn the philosophy of effort. Keen idealist as he is, he has shown a very European activity in some matters, at which even the more progressive of his countrymen stand aghast. But the reviewer has decidedly the better of his author when he sets him right in the course of his religious speculations. For instance, Mr. Malabari doubts if it is possible for the Englishman to be a Christian in the sense of " Christ's Christianity." M. Valbert retorts that it is scarcely necessary for him to be so, surrounded as he is. In the affairs of this life, religion, after all, is a matter of adaptation and accommodation. If the Christian ideal does not always fit in with the rule of conduct in the West, it does not necessarily imply the state of contradiction too readily assumed by the Eastern observer. Mr. Malabari has evidently missed this phase of the question. . . . " The Englishman has for his country the proud attachment which one has for a lawful wife that makes a great figure in the world. Mr. Malabari has for his country the tenderness that an adored mistress inspires, to whom light or morose critics deny justice, and whose weaknesses appear to the smitten heart more attractive and more lovable than the virtues of other women ".'—*Bombay Gazette*, 1894.

'A book which has the good fortune to include amongst its admirers exponents of such diverse contemporary thought as Mr. Herbert Spencer, Lord Rosebery, and Sir Alfred Lyall. We notice a new chapter on Sex. . . The marked originality, which raises incidents and details of everyday life into subjects of permanent human interest, is seldom to be mistaken, whilst the keen observation and wise counsel which abound in its pages testify to the earnestness of the social reformer. This insight into spiritual problems and the intuitive perception of religious phenomena are perhaps the chief attractions of the book for thoughtful Englishmen. . . It is only when the writer comes down to the details of domestic and social life in England that we find his grasp of the peculiarities of our robuster civilization relax, and his conclusions become sweeping. This is a serious defect in a guide usually so safe and trustworthy. But Mr. Malabari is far from dogmatic in his generalizations. Open, ingenuous, and, as a rule, careful in handling subjects with which he is not familiar, he makes allowances for what does not suit his Asiatic predilections.   Even in the worst of hypercritical moods he amuses the reader rather than offends him, the amusement sometimes being at his own expense.   The gift of humour, which singles him out for special recognition as a literary artist, never fails him in situations of difficulty that would wreck some reputations.'—*The Times of India*, 1896.

ANUBHAVIKÁ.—GUJARÁTI.

' Recognized as one of the greatest Gujaráti poets of modern times.   His latest collection of verses reveals a soul under the spell of the deep religious sense which gave birth to what was best in the Indian life and philosophy of the past, yet constrained by some power stronger than himself to break away from the past and to fix wistful eyes on the future. Under the title of *Anubhaviká*, which may not unaptly be rendered "Perceptions" or "Experiences," his poems disclose a phase of feeling through which the noblest minds in India are now passing. . .

' Mr. Malabari knows that his own faith is older than Hinduism, Christianity, or Mahommadanism, and he believes that it embodies a profounder view of the ways of God to man.   But he also realizes that whatever is to reach the Indian heart must come in an Indian guise. "After doing all that they can, the gods sit helpless in their places," runs one of his verses, which might have been written by a Hindu philosopher ; " Like a horrible shadow, thy action will follow thee always," says another, condensing the whole Buddhist doctrine of Karma into a line.   The only solutions which Mr. Malabari has to offer for the problems of existence are Duty and Work.   Throughout his poetry rings the knell of a departing world.   In it also are heard the birth-cries of a new order of things.'—*The Times*, ' Indian Affairs,' London, 1894.

THE INDIAN PROBLEM.

' Mr. Malabari has closed his present visit to England by a declaration of what he regards as the true principles of Indian progress... A remarkable document intended for English statesmen and public writers... In addition to a certain tone of unworldliness which runs through it, it is full of a gentle and conciliatory good sense which reminds one of the best examples of the Annual Epistles of the Society of Friends.   It shows that the actual facts of the India of our day are too strong alike for the political projects of the small body of Indians nurtured on Western ideals of public life, and for the disdainful attitude which some of our countrymen in India adopt towards that small educated class. .. If Mr. Malabari can help to bridge over the gulf of animosity and misunderstanding which separates these classes, he will have done an important service.'— *The Times*, ' Indian Affairs,' London, 1894.

' It is refreshing to come across a document which grasps the main situation and proceeds to point out the remedy in a statesmanlike spirit. . . . If native publicists had a tithe of the statesmanship, sobriety, and foresight shown here, the task of governing the country would be much easier than it is now.'—*The Times of India*, 1894.

' The Indian eye that saw such fascinating and good-humoured things about English life turned itself to look within India, and the result is a concise and yet graphic summary of the forces that are at work in India of to-day. A sympathetic observer, mild but keen-sighted, with firm opinions expressed in inoffensive language.'—*Indu Prakash*, 1894.

' A valuable Note on the British Administration of India ; a presentation, such as would become a true statesman, of the larger questions affecting our country. . . Mr. Malabari holds the first rank among our select native writers of English. . . In short, this Minute of Mr. Malabari's is such as to do credit to any distinguished statesman.'—*The Rast Goftar*, Bombay, 1894.

' A comprehensive survey of the various forces at work in India. Mr. Malabari writes with a candour and vigour of judgement about which there can be no mistake. His description of the situation is as felicitous as it is generally accurate.'—*The Panjab Patriot*, Lahore, 1894.

' If all our Indian reformers were actuated by the principles to which expression is given in Mr. Malabari's Memorandum, it would be a pleasure to the Anglo-Indian to encourage the movement of which he now usually entertains suspicions.'—*The Madras Times*, Madras, 1894.

' It is animated throughout with all the spirit and earnestness of a patriot and the moderation, skill, and sagacity of a statesman.'—*The Gujarât Mitra* and *Gujarât Darpan*, Surat, 1894.

'We are by no means sorry that Mr. Malabari's Memorandum has been hailed with pleasure by Anglo-Indians. The Memorandum can be read with greater profit by Anglo-Indians than Indians ; and we hope the respect and regard the former have for Mr. Malabari will induce them to treat the political reformers of this country, the educated natives, in a far kindlier spirit. . . These are noble truths clothed in unmistakable language. Are they to bear no fruit ?'—*The Madras Standard*, Madras, 1894.

' It is but natural that this wide comprehension of facts, his keen insight into character and events, his close study of the community about which he writes, and above all, the critical and impartial spirit of his remarks, should make his Memorandum acceptable, not only in the highest circles in England, but also to the Anglo-Indian community and Press in India, which do not seem to have been much respected in it. In this memorable document, Mr. Malabari approaches some of the most momentous questions in a masterly fashion ; and, though the conclusions he arrives at are not new, they are certainly well argued and clearly demonstrated.'—*The Mahratta,* Poona, 1894.

'It is most gratifying to see that, true to his convictions and to the vow he has taken to serve India most faithfully, Mr. Malabari has given us the benefit of his keen insight, shrewd observation, faithful sympathy, and his very elegant and sober style, by writing a Memorandum giving a succinct account of the political and economical situation of our country to-day; and has also stated what, in his opinion, the duty of English statesmen at present is. The Memorandum is evidently written to enlighten the upper ten of the English politicians of the day on the various vexing Indian questions. . . We heartily wish this most statesmanlike document of Mr. Malabari will be translated into every vernacular language and read by all the Indians.'—*Dnyan Prakash,* 1894.

'Owing to these reasons, also to abstaining from party squabbles, and his forbearance and impartiality, Mr. Malabari commands an amount of attention, which it is the good fortune of no other Indian publicist to obtain.'—*Bombay Gazette,* 1894.

'He has the ear of the philanthropic section of the British public. He would earn the heart-felt gratitude of the teeming and voiceless millions of this country if he could obtain financial justice for India from England.' —*Advocate,* 1894.

'All that he writes commands attention. . . There are Englishmen who know India only through Mr. Malabari and his *Spectator.* Let none complain, however. It is something to have one of us who can interpret the national will to persons in authority and can manage to be listened to. Mr. Malabari exercises a charm by his very name.'—*The Indian Nation,* 1895.